Pride Publishing books by Tom Crampton

Threads of Fate
A Different Corner

I0607448

Threads of Fate

A DIFFERENT CORNER

TOM CRAMPTON

A Different Corner
ISBN # 978-1-80250-765-2
©Copyright Tom Crampton 2024
Cover Art by Kelly Martin ©Copyright March 2024
Interior text design by Claire Siemaszkiewicz
Pride Publishing

A DIFFERENT CORNER

Dedication

This book is dedicated to my mother Anne, who instilled in me my love of words, and to Norman Stanley, who handed me the first gay novel I ever read.

Acknowledgements

My heartfelt thanks go out to the following people for their invaluable help, advice, and support during the writing of this book.

Heidi Toynbee, Sue Hidvegi, Tim Mahoney, Norma Curtis, Fi Muller, Cathy Hopkins, Bill Portlock, and Paul Thrussell.

Special thanks to my three lucky charms. Davina Rungasamy, Jack Walters, and Gabe Gane.

Thank you to everyone at Pride Publishing for their enthusiastic support and encouragement from the start.

Finally, my love and gratitude go to my eternally patient husband Charlie Gitura Yates.

Chapter One

Paddington Station was not designed for comfort. The roof was partly open to the elements so the temperature inside mimicked the outdoors. The plastic bench upon which I sat was pitted with darkened scars caused by stubbed-out cigarettes. Straight ahead, commuters gathered beneath the board detailing arrivals and departures, looking up at the clicking panels. Most had just come in from the rain and were shaking out umbrellas, fluttering like the pigeons in the rafters above. Beaded raindrops ran down faces, and people frantically searched their pockets for tickets.

He stood out to me in the midst of it all, as if he were awash with colour in a monochrome world. But judging from the flat expressions on the faces all around me, nobody else was as dazzled, and I was alone with my discovery.

He was thin and young, maybe in his mid-twenties — it was hard to tell. He wore a grubby blue shirt and black jeans, creased and well-worn. A battered rucksack hung off his back. His pale skin accentuated the shadows of exhaustion under his eyes. His unwashed, shoulder-length blond hair hung over the sides of his face, framing it like a portrait. He glanced up at the board then strolled to a bench a few metres away, cupping his chin as he leant forward to sit, elbows on his knees. I wanted to look at him, to capture an image of him, and I had to move my head repeatedly as I tried to avoid the commuters who invaded my line of vision. Then I tore my gaze away. What if he caught me staring? A few moments later I dared to look again. He was lost in a private dream. The sight of him tipped me sideways. A mere glimpse sent my stomach fluttering. Was it primal animalistic lust, or had something else about him awoken a desire deeper within me? Whatever it was, he had struck a chord.

A brusque voice from the speakers above announced that the 14:48 for Bristol was about to leave. Because I had spent the past fifteen minutes in a reverie over a stranger, I had moments to reach the platform. I wanted one last look, but he had gone. As I dashed towards the train, the engine's roar warned me that I was cutting it fine. I jumped into the nearest carriage and made my way out of first-class, through the aisles, until I was in my rightful place. A huddle of passengers waited as an elderly man struggled with his luggage, but nobody was helping him. He had a fierceness in his expression as he tried to retain his dignity. As I approached him, I offered to help, but he declined, so I went through to the next carriage where I found two empty seats.

There was a newspaper wedged down the side of one armrest, so I pulled it out and set it on the table before resting my coat and bag on the empty seat opposite, hoping nobody would sit there. The paper was folded open at a half-completed crossword, so I fetched a pen from my bag and looked at the unfinished clues. "Six across, what we 'all are architects of' per Longfellow, four letters." As I thought about this, a bag brushed against my shoulder. I didn't bother looking up.

"Is this seat taken?"

I waved with some irritation to signal the place was free and grabbed my coat and bag to clear the space. As I glanced up, my heart skipped a beat. Jerking nervously, I banged my knee and dropped my pen. It rolled under the table, and in a way that seemed no bother at all, he retrieved it from the floor.

"Thanks," I mumbled.

The whistle blew and the train shuddered forward, the engines increasing in intensity. As we picked up speed, slatted rays of watery sunlight filtered through the diesel-grimed windows of the station roof overhead. I filled in the squares with the word "fate."

* * * *

I had lived in Bath my whole life and never felt the need to stray. I was lucky to call such a beautiful city home, and I belonged there. Although it was small, there was something comforting about walking through the centre only to bump into someone I knew at any corner.

One of my earliest memories was of when my mother had first taken me to the library when I was five. There was something about that huge room that mesmerised me, the thought of all the words just waiting, ready to be devoured by my hungry mind. She held my hand as we approached the double doors, the excitement running through me as I spied the turnstile that led into the room beyond.

Behind the desk was a kind-looking lady, white hair piled high, half-moon glasses swinging from a chain around her neck. She smiled at me as my mother asked for my first library card. The librarian wore an owl-shaped brooch, its stones reflecting the light as she prepared the card for me. She explained how I could borrow any book, but I must care for it and return it on time.

This responsibility had weighed heavily on me, and, from that moment on, books had always been a treasure. Visiting the library became a ritual, and the librarian said I was their most loyal visitor. But one day, when I had just turned sixteen, she wasn't there. Knowing I would never see her again, I changed my route home so I could walk by the cemetery, still a loyal visitor. To this day, whether I was browsing in a library, a bookshop or even my own shelves at home, I could still feel my choices guided by her—she had always known what I needed to read. She had provided me with the very best literary education.

While my mother encouraged me to read, my father wanted to make sure I didn't stay in my room all day with my nose in a book. At weekends or on those balmy seventies summer evenings, we would kick a ball around Victoria Park, or play cricket or Frisbee. I loved spending time with him. He would talk to me like I was his age, telling me about his job and plans for the future. We often walked along the Royal Crescent, my hand engulfed in his warm grip, the calluses on his fingertips from years of gardening rubbing against my skin. He told me stories, inventing lands where people had wings or lived underwater, where animals talked and people never died. We often circled the park for hours, lost in tales of secret worlds beneath our feet, hidden doorways to faraway places. Not all the stories had happy endings, but that didn't matter. When I was older, I had asked him why he hadn't written the stories down. He had just shrugged and said they were for me and me only.

In the summer of '81, when I had just turned eighteen, I started working at the Bath Bookshop, where I still worked now, twelve years later. I was truly a part of the fixtures and fittings. My parents were annoyed that I didn't want to go to university, but realised I could not be dissuaded.

Even though the shop had three floors, only four of us worked there. Arthur, or "Art" as he preferred, was the owner. He had a high-pitched voice that belied his short and tubby appearance. People often gave him a second glance when he spoke. My one gripe with him was that he was far too nice. He could be over-benevolent and go a little too much out of his way for others. If any of us wanted time off, he gave it without question. Or if we were running low on cash for the month, he opened his wallet to tide us over until payday.

My other two colleagues, Ben and Tabitha, had come to work at the shop independently, then fallen in love. They had been living together for nearly eighteen months, which, by Art's reckoning, was a miracle.

Working with a partner looked suffocating. There had been far too many occasions when Art or I had to flee to a different part of the shop because the couple were in the middle of one of their heated whispered disagreements. Ben and I often went out after work for drinks, me for the company and him to escape for a while.

At thirty-five, Tabitha was older than Ben, but she looked younger than he was, as his strong face and high cheekbones aged him a bit. Her make-up was always applied with artistry and her hair styled in a different way every day, into twists and coils, or with a headscarf or polka-dot hairband. Since she was always chatty and effervescent, people confided in her, even from her position on the ground-floor till, the figurehead on the prow of the Bath Bookshop.

It had been two months since I had taken that train back from London, and only now did I want to talk about it, so I asked Ben if he wanted to go for a drink after work. He had argued with Tabitha that afternoon in the Military History section and was happy to escape for an hour. We walked past Bath Abbey and across the unfairly named Bog Island towards our local. The pub with its wooden panelling and green velvet upholstery had the vague air of a gentlemen's club, but without the aloofness. An older man nursed a large brandy at the bar. We were the only other customers. Ben and I took our usual spot at the front of the room by a large bay window.

"I don't understand her anymore. You've got the right idea sticking to the fellas," Ben said forlornly.

"Well, it's not a choice, but I know what you mean. Anyway, even though you and Tabitha argue a lot, at least you have each other."

"Sorry…"

I shrugged it off and said, "It doesn't matter. I quite like the peace and quiet of being single."

"Maybe though, just, y'know, try and get out a bit more, though? Instead of staying cooped up in your flat. Like a chicken."

I played with the rim of my pint.

"You have an elegant way of getting to the point. But, actually, I think I have met someone..."

Chapter Two

Two months ago

The rhythm of the train gave me focus as I hovered my pen over the crossword. My mind was reeling as I thought about this blond stranger in front of me. He had settled back into the seat with his rucksack resting on his knees. His eyes were closed, and his hands lay on the table, loosely clasped. I couldn't be caught staring.

His breathing was a shallow beat, his chest rising and falling beneath his shirt. I gave up on the crossword altogether and sat back. I couldn't remember the last time I had watched over someone as they dreamed...the moments when someone was at their most vulnerable. I dismissed the thought.

A lock of hair had fallen across his face, the dirty blond sparkling as sunlight filtered through the window in occasional bursts. His skin was almost translucent, which made his age even more uncertain. His fingers, long and slender, had unbitten nails, which

I envied as I compared them to my own ragged fingertips. The fine down on the back of his hands was just about discernible by sunlight. As he slept, his eyelids flickered, his nostrils flared in time with his rising chest and his lips stayed together, forbidding him from voicing his dreams.

A ripple went through the carriage as the inspector stopped at each passenger, checking the tickets. He approached our table, but the young man opposite me was sleeping soundly.

"Best wake your mate up," the inspector said to me. "I need to see his ticket, too. I'll come back."

I warily tapped the top of the stranger's hand. The sensation of his skin against mine was electrifying.

"Excuse me," I said. His eyes opened. "Sorry, but the inspector needs to see your ticket."

"I dozed off," he said with a shy smile. "Thanks for waking me."

I looked out of the window, watching the suburbs fly by and wondered what to do next. Was he one of those men who would look at me scornfully for even thinking he might be interested in a conversation? Maybe if I spoke, he would see right through it. There was something wholesome about him, though. He exuded a warmth that beguiled. I smiled for a second. Who was I kidding? I was nobody to him.

I returned my attention to the crossword.

"Given up then?" he asked, pointing at the open page.

"Be my guest," I said, a little surprised. I pushed the pen towards him. "I can't do any more."

He scanned the grid and said, "I used to do crosswords all the time when I was younger."

"They irritate me when I can't complete them. They take ages to work out sometimes," I replied.

"Ah, but that's half the fun."

"But look at some of those clues," I said. "How am I supposed to know the name of the islands situated off Port Guinea?"

"By looking in an atlas?" He ran the pen down the list of clues. "That'll be the Bissagos Islands."

I could tell from the tone of his voice that he was not trying to impress — he was simply stating the answer.

"Maybe I should read more, which is a bit ironic seeing as I work in a bookshop."

I let out a ridiculous self-conscious chuckle, and he replied, "Oh, I like people who are well read."

* * * *

"So you hit it off straight away then?" said Ben.

"He was open and friendly from the start," I said. "I bought him a tea from the trolley and everything. We spent the rest of the journey talking about all kinds of stuff."

"Oh? That sounds promising…"

"Yes, we talked about books, music and weightier topics, such as the design of the god-awful seat covers on the train."

Ben looked at his watch and sighed. "I need to get back to Tabitha."

"Yes, of course."

It was difficult to understand how volatile Ben and Tabitha could be when they were together. It was at odds with their contentment when I spoke to them separately. Not a week went by without some drama or argument. I suspected they both thrived upon it. They were polar opposites, and maybe it was their way of establishing some sort of equilibrium. I didn't think I would have the strength to deal with that in my life.

"Where is this bloke now then?" asked Ben as he put his jacket on.

"Just a few miles away. Bristol. I didn't get any more details."

"You didn't get his address or number? Your one big chance in ages, and you blew it?"

"He told me he was there just looking up some relatives. Think he's only staying for a bit."

"Is he gay? How old is he? Do you know *anything* about him at all?"

"Not really," I said, getting irritated. "Come on. I'm a complete stranger, I could hardly ask him to tell me his life story. He said his name was Daniel. Anyway, it doesn't matter. I'll probably never see him again." My voice rose a little with each word.

"Why didn't you get his number, you idiot?"

I bristled.

"Sorry. It's usually at this point that Tabitha throws something at me. Come on. Let's go."

As we walked back through town, Ben steered the conversation towards another topic. I half listened but became distracted by the fact that I would never see Daniel again, while realising Ben was right. I *didn't* know anything about this stranger. I cursed myself for acting like a teenager caught up in a fantasy about a pop star.

Ben and I parted ways, and I made my way home. I lived on the top floor of a five-storey Georgian house. The entrance hall was typically grand for such a big house, detached and impersonal. Near the foot of the staircase was a large table where the day's letters waited. I picked up my post and climbed the stairs to my flat. Among the envelopes was a flyer — there was a special night at one of the clubs. I felt I should go but had a headache that was getting stronger.

As I stepped into my flat, I called out for Ptolemy. He would usually come running, but not today. He couldn't have gone far, so I went to the bedroom to find a bulge under the duvet on my wrought-iron bed. I placed my hand on the lump and a muffled meow emerged. Ptolemy slid from under the cover, jumped onto the floor and arched his back to meet my touch as I stroked him. Picking him up, I went to the kitchen to find anything vaguely medicinal that would ease my headache. I found some paracetamol and brandished them triumphantly at my feline companion.

There was something comforting about being sequestered up high above the bustle of street life. Even though it was a cosy single-bedroom place, my home was light and airy and seemed bigger than it was. The lounge was my favourite room of all. The walls were washed in burnt ochre, decorated with old sepia photographs that had once belonged to my father. Long shelves ran along one side of the room, books stacked from floor to ceiling. Plants were scattered everywhere, their greenery resplendent against the fire-colour of the wall. The window looked out onto the splendour and elegance of the city, and most evenings, I would sit with a drink and watch the sky change its mind as it ran through its palette of colours.

Sprawled on the sofa, I relaxed as piano music drifted from the speakers. I closed my eyes and let the notes lift me into a light sleep. An hour later, my headache had vanished. The club wouldn't get busy until the pubs closed, so I cooked a meal, had a shower and chose something to wear.

It was nearly ten o'clock when I set off into the city. The streets were busy with the usual revellers and couples arm-in-arm dawdling outside shop windows as they went from restaurant to bar. I crossed the road to avoid a tribe of young men who swaggered along, filling the pavement with their jokes and slurred banter. I kept my eyes down as I increased my pace. I didn't trust them to be friendly, and I did not want to be a target. Behind them, a gaggle of shrieking girls teetered on their heels, clothed in wispy garments.

Turning up the collar of my jacket protected me against the wind and the people as I headed towards The Tap, one of the city's two gay pubs. As much as I enjoyed going out with friends, I preferred visiting the pub by myself. It took concentration and alertness to read the subtle nuances and hidden gestures between single gay men. While this might paint me as the unromantic type who, in a predatory manner, stalked gay bars in search of prey, I was, in fact, the opposite. I was completely hopeless at reading the signals. There was a fine line between self-assured confidence and complete arrogance, and some men were happy to cross it. If I ever saw a man who caught my eye in some way, instead of being flirtatious, I would just flush, then enlist the help of any friend who happened to be in the pub at the time.

In this tiny city's gay population, there were only a couple of degrees of separation, so people often knew more than they should about each other. This made it easy to glean background on an unfamiliar face if needed. I always made it a rule to know something about who I was sleeping with, especially if I had just met them that night. It didn't matter how banal this information was. The details put me strangely at ease and created a bond, so that the face and the body could become a real person. After all, who wanted to suffer the discomfort of waking up to the false caress of a stranger?

I nodded to the bouncer outside the pub. He responded with a cursory look up and down, his thick neck making him incapable of returning the nod. The music inside was frenetic and loud. Coloured lights mounted high on the walls pulsed in time with the bass, and a glitterball hung above the bar, its surface reflecting beams into the haze of dry ice that dribbled from a hidden smoke machine.

The small L-shaped room was packed. I fought my way towards the bar and waited to be noticed, eventually catching the eye of a bartender. The manager knew that hiring handsome men reaped dividends, and the staff were poured into tight-fitting clothes that showed off their gym-honed arms, which flexed proudly as the pints were pulled. Most of the punters appreciated the show, and the barmen loved the attention as they flaunted and teased their captive audience, throwing winks and smiles out like confetti. The barman handed over my drink, and I backed away through the crowd, shielding the overflowing glass from clumsy elbows. I caught sight of a friend, Owen, playing on the fruit machine. By the time I'd reached him, a good deal of beer had been spilled, and my sleeve was damp. He fed his coins into the slot and pressed the buttons, causing several flashing lights to blink wildly.

"Hold the two cherries," I said, as if I knew what I was talking about. He turned to face me with a pleased grin.

"Hellooo," he said, clapping a hand on my shoulder and kissing my cheek affectionately. "I tried ringing you the other week, but you weren't in."

"Ah, I've been busy at work," I said truthfully. "Not been out much."

Uninterested, he turned back to the machine and pressed the two buttons to hold the cherry symbols.

"Hit start," he instructed.

I did as I was told, and the third reel spun, stopping to reveal three in a row. The machine played a happy electronic melody and a bright-yellow five-pound sign flashed.

"Yes!" shouted Owen, "It's about time it started to pay out!"

He hovered his hand over the gamble button, and he turned back to me with a questioning glance.

"What the hell, live a little," I said, and leaned across to press the button again. The five-pound sign disappeared and was replaced with a ten-pound alert. He hit collect, and coins tumbled into the black plastic trough, gleaming dully. He scooped them up.

"I suppose I owe you a drink now?" he said with a pleased look. "Grab a table. I'll be right back."

I had known Owen for some years and counted him as close a friend as any. We had met here. In fact, he had tried to pick me up, but I had declined. Undaunted, he had chatted away to me anyway, and our friendship had blossomed. I often found him exhausting, as he possessed boundless energy and loved to talk, but this provided me with plenty of gossip. He was incredibly camp and the queen of put-downs. I had witnessed many guys stray into his line of fire, immediate casualties caught in the onslaught of his intentionally loud voice that cut through the music.

His chubby cheeks made it look like he still had puppy fat, despite the fact he was balding, a subject never to be discussed. In fact, he resembled an ageing schoolboy, although his current moustache and goatee marred that image a little, as did the fact he said he was in his late thirties, although I suspected he was already forty. Owen really did bring out my judgemental side.

The heat in the bar created by the thick mass of bodies was becoming oppressive, so I grabbed a table near an open window. I wiped my sleeve across a small pane to clear the condensation and looked out onto the street.

"You won't find the one out there," said Owen as he approached with our drinks.

"I'm not looking," I said, meeting his gaze with a tight smile.

"Not at the prices you charge, dear."

I took my pint from his grasp. Now was not the time to think about Daniel, as I would most certainly lapse into a maudlin state that would ruin my evening.

"So, who have you fixed your avaricious little eyes on this evening then?" I asked.

"Oh, you know," he said. "A few here and there."

He wasn't going to tell me a thing. "Oh look. There's James," he said, waving coquettishly in the direction of the door. "I'll be back in a tick."

He plunged into the crowd and made his way over to a slight young man dressed in black. Alone again, I looked around the room, self-conscious. There was a guy standing about twenty feet away with his friends. I had seen him here before. He was good looking, sporty, thick set. I guessed he was probably still in his twenties. He wore a white rugby shirt and had one hand shoved in the front pocket of his jeans a little suggestively. He turned to his friends and said something that made them laugh. He must have sensed someone was watching, as he glanced over to see if I had caught him amusing his audience. I held his gaze. I would have walked over, but his friends, a confident group of brash young twenty-somethings, put me off. I didn't move and waited until he came to me. His friends smirked and watched. As he got closer, I sipped from my glass, conscious of my fingers trembling. I held back the urge to greet him with a formal handshake.

He performed an exaggerated flourish at the empty seat opposite me. His friends had now turned away, probably content that he had reached first base. I smiled at his effrontery and gripped my pint.

"Your name's Chris, isn't it? Don't you work in the Bath Bookshop?"

"It's Christopher, and yes, I do."

"My mate thought it was you. He buys books all the time. I'm Henry."

My spirits lifted. He seemed kind, and it wasn't long before we got into a good flow of conversation. In fact, I didn't want it to stop.

"Are you going on to a club later?" I asked.

"Is that you inviting me?"

I'd never enjoyed going to clubs. I baulked at having to pay money to enter what resembled the inside of an air-raid shelter with sparse furnishings and dim, austere surroundings. The two gay clubs in town were run on a shoestring, financed by entrance fees, favours and the fact the beer was cheap. One of the clubs didn't even have a name. It had changed hands so many times that the current owners hadn't bothered. I usually went because I was dragged there by friends, only for them to spend the evening on the dance floor while I stayed at the bar, my drink, clothes and teeth shaking under the assault of basslines and hi-hats. The ferocity of the music, alienating and discordant, always shocked me into submission.

But, according to the flyer, the nameless club, which was situated under one of the pubs in the city centre, would be playing eighties music tonight, which I would enjoy. And it meant more time with Henry. As we made our way towards the club, the chill in the air cleared my mind and sharpened my senses, which had been blurred by the alcohol and heat.

"Are your friends coming later?" I pried.

"No. They're going to a party instead."

"Weren't you invited?"

"Oh yes, but I told them I had other plans…"

As we approached the anonymous doorway, two drunk men were arguing with a bouncer. Armed with overflowing kebabs, they attempted to eat as they yelled, juices and sauces dribbling off their chins and fingers. They meant nothing to the bouncer, who smiled as he saw us approaching.

"All right, lads?" he said, holding the door open for us. One of the drunks dropped his kebab on the pavement as we passed. Henry and I descended the badly lit stairwell and walked towards the booth where a bored young man smoked a cigarette.

"Eight," he muttered. I handed over a ten-pound note.

"You don't have to pay for me, you know," said Henry.

"Hey, I want to," I said, even though I resented the fee.

Pockets of people sat around the room, for now ignoring the DJ who was barricaded behind an arsenal of speakers that looked over the empty dance floor. At the other end of the room was the bar. The ceiling was inelegantly decorated with old parachutes and army camouflage webbing, creating the illusion of a militaristic harem.

"Let's go get a drink," said Henry, close to my ear.

As we leant on the bar, he moved nearer. I knew right then that the night would not end at the club. While he ordered the drinks, I took in his profile — the not-quite-straight curve of his nose, the few bristles under his chin missed while shaving and the full-bodied parted lips, which at that moment, I desperately wanted to kiss. He turned and caught me looking, but I didn't care. He put his arm around me, resting his hand in the small of my back, before letting it descend to my behind, which he squeezed once, then twice, gently.

"I take it that we have dispensed with the formal pleasantries then?" I asked.

A steady stream of people filled the club, some of whom I recognised. He was interested in who I knew, and we revelled in gossip for a while. The dance floor was getting hectic, people approaching it as if called in by a siren. Others stood on the perimeter, watching.

We found a small table in the corner and were critiquing the dancers. Owen appeared and slumped into an empty seat opposite me.

"Aren't you going to introduce me to your new friend?" he slurred.

"Henry, this is Owen. Owen, this is Henry."

Owen extended his hand to Henry, who shook it twice before absently wiping his hand on his trousers.

We attempted a conversation over the table, which was exhausting. After a while I needed to piss, but I was loath to leave them alone. As I walked away, I heard Henry asking Owen how we had met. I cringed and carried on, imagining Owen spinning an embellished tale that would probably involve him turning down my advances. By the time I had gone to the gents and made my way back, they were no longer at the table, and our seats had been taken by others. I glanced around — they were dancing among the throng on the dance floor.

Henry swayed in time to the music, his hips making small revolutions as his hands painted imaginary images. Owen was behaving himself for once. Usually he was all over his dance partner in blatant foreplay, but this time he was honouring the unspoken rule of not flirting with someone else's date.

As the DJ segued into the next song, Owen mimed to Henry that he was going to the bar. By now I had found another table, and Henry was making his way over, running his fingers through his damp hair. Faint beads of sweat gleamed on his forehead.

"I hope you didn't mind me dancing with Owen?"

"Not at all," I said, forcing a smile. "I doubt you had much choice."

"I've only been down here once before," he said, looking around. "It was a pretty shit evening. The club was half empty, and the music was crap. This is much better."

"Well, if you are up for more, I fancy a dance?" I lied because I didn't want to be outdone by Owen.

At first I was self-conscious, but soon relaxed at the familiarity of the music. We danced for an hour, and halfway through one song, Henry grabbed me by my hips, pulling me against him to tell me it was his favourite tune. His face was inches from mine. He leant closer and kissed me. His lips were like warm velvet, his tongue filling my mouth with silk. I didn't notice anyone else for the rest of the evening. I was too caught up with being the centre of Henry's affection. As soon as the club started to wind down, we left. The cold air stung my skin in a way that was pleasant after the heat of the club. With hands thrust deep in pockets and shoulders hunched against the chill, we headed towards my flat.

Chapter Three

People have different perceptions of what it might be like to live alone. Some imagine a quiet life filled with contemplative monk-like silence. Others imagine a scenario where a pariah has been cast out from society, a misfit, shunned and lonely. Then there are those who think it makes a statement to break away from what is considered normal. But, more often than not, those who conjure up the stereotypes never pause to think *why* a person might choose to live alone.

Five years ago, at the age of twenty-five, I had thought I was too young to settle down with anybody. I'd had a few boyfriends over the years but never anything serious. I hadn't ever fallen in love and was careful about how much of myself I gave to one person. In all these casual trysts, none of the men had ever said they wanted to take things further.

The idea of being tethered to somebody had struck me as ludicrous. I had still been young and wanted to wallow and luxuriate in the diverse groups of people I met or was yet to meet. There was something so very final about settling down, almost retiring from a journey. I had been happy to pause and catch my breath, but I still had a long way to travel. At twenty-five, I had lived with my parents, but I had craved solitude and spent many evenings in my room reading. However, I enjoyed the company of friends, especially for a meal or drinks. At that age, I had been skipping my way through life, unaware that things were about to change.

My parents had gone to Bristol to watch a show at the Old Vic, a treat they had enjoyed frequently over the twenty-seven years they had been married. They said it would have been quick. They did not suffer. It was a head-on collision with a drunk driver on a dual carriageway.

Afterwards, like a chrysalis held in the security of a family's heart, I struggled to be reborn, casting away the skin of my old life, facing a future on my own. Losing both parents at the same time was a shock that nobody could ever recover from. I learnt to numb the pain, but it sometimes resurfaced, usually in the dead of night, crippling my confidence and reminding me that deep down, I was a terrified little boy who was all alone in the world.

I had all the love and support I needed from relatives, both distant and near. My uncle had handled everything. I only had vague memories of the months that came after. Art had told me to take time off and come back when I was ready. My uncle had helped me navigate the maze of legalities that followed. I had found myself with a considerable amount of money, so I bought my flat. Now, five years later, I was beginning to place my feet back on that path I had strayed from. Occasionally, I would stop and turn around to see if my father was waiting there for just one more story in the park or if my mother would approach me with her arms outstretched, ready for another cherished visit to the library.

As I made the gradual change from thinking of myself as an orphaned child to being an adult whose parents were no longer living, I ruminated about the yearnings I had towards men. But this was not just about the physical pursuit of sex — it was a craving for intimacy of a different sort. Although I had thought about the joys of a relationship, I just couldn't commit to sharing my life fully and openly with someone. Where would I escape to when I wanted to be alone? I wouldn't want to run away and leave someone hurt. I had once broached this with Owen. He told me that life was too short and to shut up and enjoy myself. I thought he had a point.

I closed the door of my flat and listened to Henry's footsteps as he went down the steps to the entrance hall below. Putting my fingers to my swollen lips, bruised by his fierce kissing, I noticed Ptolemy looking at me with disapproval. I cleared the detritus from the previous evening. The cushions from the sofa were cast over the floor, and wine bottles and dirty glasses lay empty on the coffee table. Henry had left to go home and nurse his aching head, but I had to be at the bookshop in a couple of hours. Saturdays were busy, and unless my headache cleared, I was in for a very long day.

I fed the cat, took paracetamol and walked to the bathroom, where Henry's presence was still apparent. A damp towel hung on the towel rail. I pulled off my underwear, which I had put on in my hungover, half-hearted attempt at modesty this morning when I had gone to make coffee. I stepped into the shower and closed my eyes, the needles of the spray making me alert. Away from the harsh glare of the ceiling lights, which reflected brightly against the white tiles, I washed my hair and turned up the heat to as much as I could bear.

The bedroom smelled of sweat and sex. I opened the window to let in air. The bed looked like it had seen better days. The duvet and sheets were knotted into a rumpled pile, the victim of last night's exertions. As I stripped the bed, I noticed a note on the bedside table. Henry had left me his number. I picked it up and traced the numerals. He had added his name at the top.

We had stumbled in at just past two this morning and gone straight to the lounge, where I turned down the lights and lit a couple of candles instead. Collapsed on the sofa, we had drunk wine and chatted. The alcohol consumed and the late hour had created an atmosphere that hung heavy with anticipation of what was to come.

I remember opening another bottle of wine.

"We're going to have bad heads in the morning if we continue drinking," he had said.

"I think we passed that stage a while ago."

"I'll have another if you join me."

"I will if we go somewhere more comfortable?"

Without waiting for him to reply, I grabbed the wine bottle and glasses and walked towards the bedroom. He followed me, and I closed the door firmly behind us.

Once inside, Henry turned towards me and kissed my lips. He placed his arms around me and slowly pulled me closer inside his embrace. He undid a couple of buttons on the front of my shirt, then slid his warm hands inside, roaming over my chest, pausing to caress a nipple then stroking down my midriff towards my belt.

A sigh escaped me as Henry removed my shirt and pushed me down onto the bed, where he proceeded to kiss my chest, dampening each nipple and the sparse hair around them. I struggled under his weight to sit upright so I could pull his rugby shirt up and over his head. The soft streetlight through the bedroom window highlighted the swell of his pectoral muscles. A light matting of black chest hair covered them and continued farther down his body. I greedily ran my hands through it, relishing the silky texture against the hard flesh beneath. We were both breathing more heavily. Now firmer and more urgent in my actions, I pulled Henry down on top of me, the heat from his body suffusing mine. Not one word was uttered, just indecipherable whispers and hot breath in my ear as Henry rubbed himself against me. Our kisses grew more fervent and our movements bolder as we explored each other's bodies with an intimate, animalistic intensity.

Henry reached down and tugged at my belt, trying to undo the clasp. I helped him, then reached over and did the same to his, feeling an obvious bulge straining beneath the fabric of his jeans. We stood to finish removing each other's trousers and discarded our underwear. Falling onto the bed, we writhed and groped each other in a clumsy embrace. Henry pinned my arms above my head and started to explore my body with his tongue. He would always return to my mouth, plunging his tongue inside, his stubble rasping against my lips like sandpaper. Straddling me, he reached down and grabbed our hard cocks together in one hand. I was moaning now and leant up so I could once more fuse my mouth to his. Henry slid his fist up and down, the speed increasing. I groaned as the pleasure mounted, sucking on his probing tongue.

Then with the clarity of a note ringing from a bell, the image of Daniel's face registered in my head. We each shuddered as our orgasms overtook us.

Shaking with exertion, Henry collapsed on top of me, our pooled fluids on my chest and stomach gluing us together. Even drunk, the guilt was immediate. Why had Daniel come to mind at that exact moment?

I lay there and held Henry, rubbing my hand up and down his back. His breathing started to slow in rhythm. After pushing him off me and rolling him onto his back, I grabbed a towel and wiped us both clean. I climbed back into bed and pulled the duvet over us both. Henry murmured his thanks, his voice slurred and eyes closed. He rolled on his side towards me, throwing an arm out and over my chest. He pulled me closer, and I fell from grace into a dreamless sleep.

Chapter Four

It was in those hours after work, when the evening was stretched out, waiting to be filled, that I thought about turning to my partner and asking, "What shall we do tonight?" Sharing that time was something I had started yearning for, but this longing for companionship was also needling me. As I waited for Art to stop fumbling with the locks on the shop door, I looked forward to spending the evening curled up on the sofa with a book. My sexual appetite had been satisfied by last night's activities, and I needed a quiet night in. Art said goodbye, and I watched him walk away. His gait was reminiscent of a child who had just started to walk, his legs unsteady under his portly frame. As he went round the corner, the glare from a car's headlights illuminated his outline. Art always admired others for what was within. He was also the least judgemental person I knew and could bring out the best in people. Because of what had happened to my parents, he had taken to mothering me from afar, but it never felt too much. He was always available in a crisis, and it was comforting to know someone cared.

I walked home, a lightness in my step. I wouldn't go out tonight. Staying in meant no lounging against the bar, no feigning interest in some stranger's monologue, nodding in all the right places while they enjoyed the sound of their own voice. I revelled in the silence of my own company. I knew that reading a book for hours on end would not find me a partner, but neither did I want to go out every night with desperation etched across my face for others to pity. I was in a quandary — I hadn't reconciled myself to the thought that I might be ready for a serious relationship and all the complexities it would entail.

As I entered the flat, Ptolemy wrapped himself around my legs, chirruping and purring. I ran my fingers along his back through his soft fur. We went through this routine most days, and so far neither of us had tired of it. Ptolemy had belonged to my parents. Because he was a rescue cat, we had never known how old he was, but his fur was now greying in places, and he was not as limber as he used to be.

After I had eaten, I placed fresh sheets on the bed and washed the dishes. Satisfied, I settled on the sofa with a novel. I woke up several hours later, still on the sofa. It was half one in the morning. I had barely read a word. Groaning at the stiffness in my back and irritated at myself, I got up and went to bed. Too tired to fold my clothes, I hung them from the chair. I climbed into bed, and Ptolemy jumped up to join me, curling up into a ball near my feet. I fell asleep, my mind echoing his faint purr of contentment.

I awoke the next morning feeling refreshed. Unlike most Sundays, my head wasn't pounding, and my mouth didn't taste bitter. Ptolemy still slept, his whiskers twitching as he dreamed. I savoured the silence and the thought of a day of leisure. In the lounge, I pulled up the blinds and let the sun flood in. The windows were recessed into the thick wall, and I often sat on the sill and watched the world drift by. The view looked out over the hills of Bath, while below lay a garden. Beyond that was the tree-lined Gravel Walk, a path that ran in one direction towards the splendour of the Royal Crescent.

I lifted the pane of the sash window, expecting a cold breeze to come through, but instead I received a warm sensation tinged with the scent of blossom. From my eyrie in the sky, I observed as the people ambled by, unaware of my presence. A couple, arm-in-arm, drifted past below. In their small world, they only had eyes for each other. I wondered how they had met and what had attracted them to each other. Strolling behind them was a young woman with a baby in a pushchair. Was she a single mother, or was her husband at work? Or did she have IVF, so she could start a family with her girlfriend? I wanted to know all their stories.

The phone in the kitchen sounded, breaking me out of my reverie. I rushed to pick it up.

"Christopher, it's Oliver."

"Ollie! It's been ages."

He paused, then giggled. He only rang when he wanted to share something outrageous, a wild story he hoped would make me jealous, despite the fact it seldom did.

"What's so funny?"

"So, I went to the pub last night for the first time in ages and picked up an incredibly cute guy…"

"How old was he?"

"*Young,*" he replied. "And hot."

His ability to always pick up new men was annoying, but his bragging irritated me more.

"Well, that's nice."

"So, I'm inviting you out for a drink with us this lunchtime."

"And why would I want to do that?" I tried not to sound intrigued.

"Well, I'm not sure if this one is actually gay or not."

"You pick up a guy in a gay pub, and you don't know if he's gay or not?"

"He seemed interested when I was chatting to him. But back at mine, things changed."

I began to enjoy the conversation a lot more.

"After we had a couple of drinks, I, you know, sat a bit closer to him."

"Uh-huh."

"He said he was tired, and would I mind if he slept on the *sofa*, would you believe?"

He sounded appalled, which made me stifle a laugh.

"So what did you do?" I asked with fake concern. "I bet you were furious."

"There wasn't much I could fucking do, was there? It was one in the morning, so I couldn't exactly throw him out on the street. I suppose I could have called a taxi. Anyway, I got a blanket and bloody left him to it. I went to bed."

He would have been truly pissed off if I told him about my night with Henry.

"So you want me to come for a drink to try and figure out if this guy is interested in you?"

"Yes, please," he replied.

"All right, I'll come."

I had met Oliver at a dinner party some years ago and taken a dislike to him due to his inherited wealth that had made him act superior and brashly confident. He had monopolised the dinner with his stories that night, making it clear that he had already achieved more in his forty-five years than most people would in their lifetimes. The places he had been rolled off his tongue, cities I hadn't even heard of. His love of art was an obsession, and he had opened four successful galleries across Europe, including one in London. With his name established in the art world, he had turned his attention to social standing and, at the age of thirty-three, had married Sophia, an Italian socialite.

A year later, they had divorced. She had returned from a trip to Florence a day early to surprise him, only to find him in bed with a young man. The surprise was all on her. Oliver had recounted his version of events to us during the dinner party, and it had left me exhausted.

He had used theatrical gestures as he told us the tale. "As quickly as she entered our Hampstead residence that day, she walked out, her lips pressed into a hard slash as she saw me naked with a sheet clutched to my torso, the outline of my lover behind me in the shadows. I rushed through the apartment to plead with her, but, tearful and enraged, she wanted nothing more to do with me."

I'd leant back in my chair and looked around at the other guests, who were hanging on to every word of his story, entranced. Playing with other people's affections seemed a game to him, a momentary diversion, and the gleeful way in which he described the scene had filled me with distaste.

"Are you still in touch with either of them?" I'd asked, interrupting him mid-flow.

His glacial blue eyes had regarded me coolly. I'd seen the flash of irritation in them as he met my gaze.

"No, I don't believe I am," he'd replied after a pause.

I'd nodded politely, thinking that I doubted he could even remember the young man's name. Throughout the rest of the meal, I would catch him stealing the occasional glance at me, his brow furrowed. I might have committed some social faux pas by interjecting during his self-indulgent monologue, but by that point, I'd heard enough. I certainly wasn't impressed by his unabashed hedonistic approach to life, but maybe that said more about me.

Our paths had crossed again when he had opened a gallery in Bath and bought a flat in the city. I got to know him more as he started drinking down at The Tap. Since the collapse of his marriage and admitting to himself that he wasn't in any way straight, he had devoted his spare time to seducing young men with a fervour that was almost religious in nature. Sex was never on the cards between us, though. I had made that perfectly clear during one social event where he had suggested he'd like to take things further. Still, we had something — and I wouldn't call it friendship — I didn't think either of us could explain why we kept in touch or why we occasionally had a drink together — but I thought he admired my indifference to his lifestyle. He was intelligent, loved his work and enjoyed the trappings that went with it. My fridge door was papered with postcards he had sent from various exotic locations.

I walked for forty-five minutes along the Avon until I reached the riverside pub. There was no sign of him or his friend, so I bought a drink and went to the lawn where people were sitting at tables close to the water. The chatter and the chink of ice cubes provided a relaxing chorus that paired with the scent of the cut grass. At the far end of the lawn, I saw two figures sitting, one upright, the other more reposed. As I approached, Oliver spotted me and beckoned me with a wave. I tried to focus against the glare of the sun. As the sun disappeared behind a cloud, I glimpsed his friend. I tried to keep it together. Drawing level, I could tell Oliver was nervous. It was strange seeing him like this. With a slight waver in his voice, he said, "This is Daniel."

"Hi, I believe we've met," said Daniel with a cheeky look.

Oliver looked confused.

"A couple of months ago," I said to him. "Travelling back from London." I leant forward to shake Daniel's hand.

"It's good to see you again," he said. "And by the way, I finished your crossword."

There was rising irritation in Oliver's expression, which I countered with an angelic smile.

"Small world, isn't it?" he muttered to me. Daniel seemed oblivious to the tension.

"How come you're in Bath?" I asked. "You said on the train you were staying in Bristol?"

"I've been here with work this week. The rest of the time I've been in Bristol, looking up family, visiting friends."

"What line of work are you in?" asked Oliver.

"Oh, you know, casual stuff like bar work."

It was no surprise Oliver was asking this now — he preferred to talk about himself rather than listen to others.

"You work in a bookshop, don't you?" Daniel said.

Oliver rolled his eyes.

"You've got a good memory," I replied.

"Maybe, but can you remember the name of the islands in the crossword clue?"

"The Bissagos Islands..."

Oliver glowered, then said, "I've been to the Bissagos Islands. They're beautiful this time of year."

Of course you have, Oliver. Then it was as if Daniel had read my mind, because he laughed, catching my gaze. Oliver was delighted to have regained control of the conversation, not quite realising he was being mocked. We listened as he told us about his time on the islands, but I couldn't quite believe the subject of my thoughts for the past two months was here, right opposite me. I felt as if I were floating above, watching events unfold. Was Daniel aware of how much I wanted him? Could he read it in my body language? When our eyes met, I wanted him to see the real me hiding inside.

I desperately wanted to talk to Daniel. There were so many questions that I'd rehearsed in my head to ask, but Oliver was on a roll, and as usual, was monopolising the conversation. I concentrated on what was being said, not wanting to miss anything. I was determined to commit any of Daniel's words to memory, so I could replay them in my head later and check for any nuances.

"...flew direct into Munich to meet an art dealer, then east to Vienna to attend an exhibition. I managed a few hours' sleep on my flight to Turin, where I'm thinking of opening a gallery. It was an exhausting weekend, but I made around fifty grand, so it wasn't all bad."

Oliver drained his drink and glanced at our glasses. "Who's for another?"

He snapped his fingers at a member of staff who was clearing a nearby table. The young man looked around, eyebrows raised.

"Could we get some more drinks over here?"

I glanced at Daniel, who looked embarrassed. He shook his head and stared down at his lap.

"Sir, you need to order your drinks at the bar."

Oliver muttered something under his breath and beckoned the young man over with an impatient flourish of one hand, while the other reached inside his jacket and withdrew a wallet. When he opened it up, plainly visible was a fat wad of cash. Oliver peeled off a fifty-pound note and held it out to the staff member, who stood clutching some empty glasses, looking uncertain and shifting his weight from one foot to the other before reaching out to take the money.

"Two gin and tonics and another bottle of lager." Oliver gave the youth a rictus grin, which didn't suit his face at all. "Oh, and keep the change." He turned his attention back to us, dismissing the staff member entirely.

"Where was I? Ah yes, Turin. Have either of you ever been?" He didn't wait for us to answer. "I'm always on the lookout for new artists. Found this girl there who's only in her mid-twenties. Gorgeous little thing. She makes bronze sculptures. Absolutely exquisite. I offered to buy her entire collection. I always have buyers lined up, you see. Anyway, she refused. Apparently they're symbolic of her cultural identity, and she didn't want them to leave Italy." He snorted with what sounded like contempt. "So what did I do?" Daniel shook his head politely.

"I stormed out of her little workshop, shouting over my shoulder in Italian that art is global, darling. Her face was a picture. I've arranged for a local dealer to buy them for me. I'll have them soon enough." He shrugged. "Sometimes you have to be a bit of a bastard in this game. If you don't keep your wits about you, someone else will beat you to it. That reminds me of a time in London when I met this Egyptian guy..."

I had heard it all many times. For someone who made an obscene amount of money and voyaged the world, he made it sound like a real burden. However, none of it seemed to be working on Daniel. He waited until Oliver paused for breath before interjecting.

"That's too bad," he said. "I suppose I've got it lucky working till two in the morning every day, having to serve drunks who don't like waiting for their next drink or blokes looking for trouble and an excuse for a fight. If I'm really lucky, I might have to clean up someone's puke in the bathroom."

Oliver shifted in his seat.

"That sounds pretty taxing," I said.

"It is," said Daniel. "But it has its good points, you know — free drinks, live music and *most* of the customers are pretty cool."

Oliver backed down and stopped trying so hard. It was as if he was learning how to have a proper conversation for the first time. We chatted for a while before Daniel announced he had to meet a friend in town.

Without missing a beat, Oliver reached for his jacket. "I'm going that way myself. I'll drop you off."

"How about you, Christopher?" said Daniel. "Coming with us?"

Oliver rolled his eyes.

"Sure." I drained my glass.

We took the short walk in silence to Oliver's sleek two-door BMW.

"New wheels?" I asked.

"Yeah, I thought it was time for something more updated," he said, unlocking the silver car.

I held the door open for Daniel, but he gestured for me to go in first, so I folded the seat forward and clambered into the back. It wasn't comfortable. Daniel lowered himself into the front seat, leaving me free to study the elegant line of his neck and shoulder. The car started, and Oliver revved the engine a few times, before saying, "You'll like this, watch."

He pressed a button on the dashboard, and the roof opened, settling back behind my head. Daniel looked impressed.

"Boys and their toys," I said.

"That's nothing. Wait till we get out on the road."

We roared out of the car park and took the short journey back to the city centre. Daniel seemed in his element, his arm hanging outside the open window. His golden hair whipped back. I wondered if this kind of life was something he wanted. True, it was hard not to feel exhilarated travelling at speed, exposed to the elements, so I sat back to enjoy it for these few brief minutes. We pulled up at my flat, and Daniel stepped onto the pavement to let me out. The midafternoon sunlight illuminated the honeyed Bath-stone bricks.

"Which one's yours?" he asked.

I gestured towards my windows.

"Looks pretty nice."

"It is. I just own the flat on the top floor, though. That's all I need. I like being up high. It's a good place to think."

"Maybe I'll see you around, then?" he said. I shook his hand, taking in the warmth of his skin.

Oliver leaned across the passenger seat to interrupt. "I'll give you a call in a day or so, okay, Chris?"

Daniel crouched back into the car and slammed the door shut. The engine gunned as the car roared up the road. I stood outside on the pavement for a moment, unsure of everything that had just passed. It seemed like a glimpse. Had it even happened? I cursed as, yet again, like sand, Daniel slipped through my fingers. I opened the door to my building and walked in before hesitating. Did I want to slam the door or let it quietly close itself? A neighbour came in and took the decision away from me, and as we walked up the stairs, I could still feel Daniel's palm in mine.

Chapter Five

All I wanted to do today was bury myself in work so I didn't have to think about Daniel and Oliver. I'd spent the rest of Sunday brooding, unsettled, pacing around my flat. My cravings for the attention of a loving partner were starting to prey on my mind, but like an itch I was unable to scratch, this desire was becoming an irritation. No one would be attracted to a desperate man—I realised that, not that I imagined myself smiling at anyone who looked my way. Lonely I might have been, but pathetic and without dignity I was not. But whenever I started my solitary walks home after a night out, the journeys seemed to last longer each time.

At some point on Sunday, I caught my reflection in the hallway mirror. I paused for something I rarely did. I looked straight at myself and met my own gaze. My reflection stared back, daring me to call its bluff. I found it disconcerting to hold my image in thrall for too long. My mousy brown hair was showing its first signs of retreat, and I had a dusting of stubble over my chin and cheeks. When I was a child, I would trace my fingers over my father's stubble, fascinated by the prickly coarseness. I passed my fingers over my own jaw, dismayed at how fleeting the time was from sitting on my father's knee until now. It seemed so transitory, the key part he had played in my life. A small scar lay half hidden in the dimple of my chin, a reminder of a childhood accident. Creasing my face into a grimace, I analysed my eyebrows, my nose, my ears, my cheekbones. Nothing rendered me a monster, though it certainly was no Adonis appraising me in return. This version of myself was always there when I needed him. I could ask his advice, share a self-doubt, whisper a secret or trade a knowing smile.

Although I was feeling low, I was no longer at war with myself. My evening of soul-searching had done me good. Gaining the confidence to like who I was made the journey to find someone seem much easier. Daniel had slipped through my fingers because of my own temporary lack of faith. I would not make the same mistake again. It was just the ache of wanting him that made me miserable, and the understanding that I might never see him again. I hadn't asked Daniel where he was working, but I would try to get the information from Oliver with a few casual, innocent-sounding enquiries. It was either that or trawl around every bar in the city, hoping for a glimpse.

The next morning at work, a huge delivery of books arrived, and I was tasked with unpacking the contents and putting them in the correct places across all three floors. It would take most of the day, but I was glad of the distraction. Ben and Tabitha seemed happy enough working together today. Sometimes it was exhausting listening to them squabble, especially as they were so unaware of how public they could be. It was unprofessional to bring problems to work, but it was also a place where they could air grievances and come to a compromise. These disagreements happened so much that it made me thankful not to be in a relationship, if that was what it entailed. I knew they were an extreme example, but respect and understanding had to be there from both sides if any couple wanted to be truly happy. It was plain Ben and Tabitha loved each other, but they were suffocated by always being together. It sounded like hell.

The routine of work gave me comfort. I looked at the time. It was nearly ten o'clock, so Mrs Willis, a tiny old lady who browsed as quiet as a mouse, would be in soon. Belying her size, she had a murderous appetite for crime novels, and each week she left with an assortment of hardbacks to last her till the following week. Mondays also heralded the arrival of old Bagley, a bad-tempered man whose gruff demeanour commanded respect, as years serving his country had ingrained an unyielding rigidity to his persona. Naturally he only ever bought books about military history, although Tabitha once reckoned he had snuck some erotic fiction into his selection.

Another regular, Maggie, had just come into the shop. She had never taken to me, but adored Tabitha. Still, I tried.

"Hi, Maggie. How are you today?" I asked.

She stiffened at the mention of her name, then turned back to the window, where we currently had a George Orwell display.

"Before she retired, my mum was a nurse at the 'ospital in London where 'e died. She never cared for who 'e was."

Maggie had come to Bath from London a long time ago and often pitched up in a prime position just down the road from the bookshop for the city's tourists to drop pennies into her hat. In hot weather, we regularly filled up her dog's water bowl. I reached down to scratch Bonnie on her grey grizzled muzzle. She licked my hand.

"We read a bit of Orwell at school," I said, not quite knowing how to reply.

"I read some of 'is now, never at school. When my mate's around, 'e looks after Bonnie, see, an' I go the library to read."

She smiled with what I thought was a trace of sadness. Her lean face was kind and wise. People in Bath always kept an eye out for Maggie and made sure she was all right. She was always kept rich with donated books, too.

She looked me up and down, then said, "You spend too much time inside." She walked off to find Tabitha, who often passed her own books on to Maggie.

* * * *

At lunchtime, Maggie's words were still on my mind. She was right – I did spend too much time inside. What was there to be discovered never leaving the confines of the places that made me feel most at home? It was a nice day, so rather than sit in the staff room, I wandered outdoors and passed Maggie's pitch. She wasn't there, but she was sitting opposite, reading, with Bonnie sleeping on a cushion beside her. I reached into my bag and placed the sandwiches I had made this morning next to her in gratitude.

I barely noticed as the days segued into the other, the minutiae of work and home repeating. On Wednesday, as I made my way to work, heavy sheets of rain pounded the pavement with an unrepentant fury. I unfurled my umbrella to brave the weather, but despite the rain, my spirits were buoyant. I had somehow dragged myself out of the well of self-pity that I had fallen into earlier in the week. I let myself into the shop, and Art looked up from the counter. "Someone looks happy," he said. "Have you fallen in love?"

I laughed at the irony of this throwaway phrase he often used. Tabitha arrived moments later. "Morning," she said, her face stony. She walked towards the staff room, with Ben following. At the last minute, he had a change of heart and hung back.

"I'll go," said Art and went after Tabitha.

"I'm not even going to ask," I said to Ben, as he slung his drenched coat behind the counter. There was a faint scuff on his left cheek.

"You're not going to believe this," he said.

"Try me."

He pushed back his fringe, revealing what turned out to be a nasty bruise.

"Tabitha's mother's coming to visit for a few days, yeah? When Tab told me, I realised it clashed with something I'm doing with my mates."

"Can't you cancel?"

"No, I'm meant to be going to a gig. Anyway, I already paid for the bloody tickets. Thing is, she didn't even tell me her sodding mother was coming down, and then she blames me for arranging something behind her back."

I didn't care. I was sick of absorbing the stress of other people's failures to maintain a happy relationship. The day had hardly started, and already I wanted to be in the sanctuary of my flat with Ptolemy.

"So that bruise is proof neither of you found a solution?"

"She threw a shoe at me!"

I tried to look sympathetic, but my instinct was to laugh. She could have hurt him, but I could tell this was about so much more, a bubbling over of too many fights and arguments. The staffroom door opened, and Art emerged. "Ben, there's a mug of tea waiting for you in the staff room. Christopher, hold the fort."

Ben slunk in Art's direction, his face flushed. Once Ben had passed through the door, Art looked at me, raising his hands towards the ceiling, as if supplicating himself to some divine power that would grant him the strength to sort this all out. I had no idea why Art felt the need to get involved. Maybe it was just to keep the peace at work.

Ben and Tabitha's relationship seemed to thrive on altercations like these, but this was the first time that I knew of where violence had been involved. I unlocked the front door and put some music on, glad to be alone. Twenty minutes later, the three of them appeared. Art had affected an air of breeziness and sent Ben and Tabitha to different floors armed with tasks. The atmosphere remained tense and strained throughout the morning, but by late afternoon, unlike outside, the weather inside had blown over, and Art could trust the couple to work together again.

"They act like bloody kids sometimes," Art said to me later in his office. He lit a slim cigar. "They were too busy quarrelling instead of coming up with an answer.

I told them I wouldn't tolerate any more personal problems being brought to work."

Finally. I couldn't believe he had put up with it for so long.

The blue silvery cigarette smoke poured from his nostrils, as if he were exorcising a malevolent spirit from within. It curled up, eddying around towards the air-conditioning vents overhead.

"That doesn't sound like the Art I know," I said.

"Well, sometimes enough is enough."

He only smoked when he was stressed. I wanted to tell him about Daniel, explain how I held this person in such thrall, although we had only met twice. Art was good at steering me along the right path, but I was conflicted, because Oliver was infatuated with Daniel, although it seemed unreciprocated. Would I be crossing a line by trying to establish contact? It was frustrating not having the answers, but it was clear that now was not a good time. I decided to wait before I asked Art for advice.

The rain persisted, the occasional customer bringing damp footprints into the shop. When the weather was this bad, so was the trade. People only ventured in if they wanted to seek shelter from the elements. We ended up closing early. Ben and Tabitha left first, forced to huddle together under a shared umbrella, seeking comfort in each other. As I walked through the city, I looked up at the sky and saw nothing but the heaviness of clouds. People scurried along the street, crouched, as if the sky was in danger of touching their heads. The slap of feet on the puddles sent splashes up legs, dampening hems and ruining shoe leather. I rushed round the corner to the Circus, a circular road lined by tall Georgian houses. In the middle, the huge imposing plane trees swayed angrily in the wind, the leaves glowing with a fresh lurid intensity. Their limbs creaked and groaned, and I could imagine them snapping loose, like a sail ripping free from rigging in a storm. The wind whipped the rain across my face, as I turned into Brock Street. I felt bullied by the elements, the rain dripping off the edge of my nose adding to the torment.

As I approached my building, I spotted a black bin liner filled with rubbish slung against the door and was immediately irritated by it. But, getting closer through the haze of the rain, I saw it was a person slumped in the doorway. The figure was motionless. I had a dreadful fear they might be dead. Their head was covered with a sopping wet hood, so I couldn't know for sure. I moved in closer, my splashes loud and clear. This seemed to prompt the figure into life, and they dropped their hood.

"Daniel... What the hell?"

When I had seen him in the pub, he had been so cool and lively, but now it was a shock to see him hunched and grey as the cold penetrated his body.

"I had nowhere else to go," he said, his voice cracking.

I helped him to his feet and, with my arm around him, we walked up the stairs, our shoes squeaking on the floor tiles. In my flat, he stood in the hallway dripping onto the carpet, wiping water from his eyes and face. Ptolemy did not look impressed.

"You should get out of those wet clothes."

"Yeah..."

He had nothing with him, no bag or rucksack.

"Take a shower to warm up if you like?"

As soon as I said it, I felt as if I'd overstepped the mark.

"Thank you, but it's okay. It's rude of me just appearing on your doorstep like an abandoned baby."

I laughed.

"A towel would be good, though."

I went to find a clean one and decided to grab some clothes, too. He was the same build as me, but maybe two or three inches taller. I got some old jeans and a cotton shirt, before hesitating — was it too intimate to include underwear? Anxiety started to get the better of me as I tried to make sense of the past few minutes, questioning why he had chosen my doorstep. He was a lot more fragile than I had thought. It wasn't even six o'clock — not an hour had passed since I had left work, yet it seemed like days had gone by. I went back and handed him the towel and clothes.

"I'll make us some tea."

I took my time, watching as the steam from the kettle waved the notes and reminders that were pinned on my noticeboard. The sight of Henry's number curling sent a twinge of guilt through me. What was the etiquette when it came to calling back a hastily scribbled number? After the thrill of the night had faded, the next day often crept in with rationality. Henry was a nice guy. Maybe I should call him next week. When it seemed enough time had passed, I took the mugs through to the living room. Daniel was standing at the far wall in his borrowed trousers, which stopped well above his ankles. His damp hair was swept back, and colour had returned to his cheeks.

"Here you go," I said, setting down the tea.

He was examining the old sepia photos that hung on the wall.

"These are beautiful," he said. "Where did you get them?"

"They belonged to my father."

"Oh?"

"Yes, he collected them over a few years. I never looked at them much growing up, because he kept them stashed away. I don't understand why he didn't hang them up."

Daniel moved from image to image. There were eighteen photos on the wall, but I had six more albums in my attic. The pictures, all contained within dark wooden frames, were an eclectic mix. Some were of people from a century ago, unaware they had been immortalised as they went about their day. Buildings and storefronts formed the backdrop to a glimpse of Parisian street life in the 1930s. Large gnarled driftwood stood sentry on a deserted Venezuelan beach. An abandoned temple in Pakistan stood waiting for nature to reclaim it.

"I like this one," Daniel said, pointing to an image of a paddle steamer on the Missouri River. It was taken from an elevated position on the bank and showed the boat making its way through the water, the steam echoing the froth in the boat's wake. Etched in the corner of the picture in shaky handwriting was "1864". It was my favourite. The pictures came together to create one piece of art, and over time, I had begun to understand why my father had liked them so much, the sepia tones romanticising and blurring the colours of everyday life.

"Daniel, I have to ask, but are you okay?"

"Not really." He traced a picture frame with one finger. "I've been staying at the YMCA. When I woke up this morning, my wallet and rucksack had been nicked. The only thing I have is my passport. I sleep with it under my pillow."

He sat on the wide windowsill and looked through the rain-splashed pane. I took the chair opposite, ready to hear what else he had to say.

Chapter Six

After breakfast, Daniel and I walked through Royal Victoria Park. The night before, he had stayed on the sofa, as he must have done the night he'd met Oliver. We ambled along the pale-yellow gravel paths, and although he hesitated at first, soon his voice found a rhythm and flow as he told me his story.

"I grew up in Dartford, just outside London. My parents split up when I was fourteen. My dad took a job abroad." Daniel glanced at me to check I was listening. "I never really saw him much growing up, so it didn't make much difference to me, but my mum's world fell apart. It was horrible to watch."

I nodded, willing him to continue.

"You'd like her. I know she would like you. Her name's Joanna." Daniel paused. The sound of the gravel crunching beneath our feet filled the air. "She started drinking," he said matter-of-factly. "Sometimes she would have men round. I used to do everything I could to avoid going home. I'd kill time by hanging out in the local park or stay with friends after school."

I thought of my own cosseted upbringing. It didn't compare.

"Don't get me wrong," Daniel added hastily. "I wasn't unloved, and I didn't go without. It was just that over the next few years, Mum changed. She used to be so house-proud and always quick to laugh. I didn't realise she had money troubles until we were forced to move to a tiny flat in a rough part of town."

"Did things get better?" I asked, hoping that at some point their fortunes had changed.

Daniel shook his head. "Not really. I was doing well at school and ended up going to Bristol University to study history. It was meant to be an exciting time, but I was worried about leaving my mum alone. I was angry and hurt that my dad had abandoned us. I couldn't discuss him with her. She wouldn't even allow his name to be mentioned."

We stopped for a moment to watch a woman throw a ball for her springer spaniel. Its ears flapped as the dog ran at breakneck speed, its tongue hanging out of the side of its mouth.

"Did you enjoy university?" I asked.

Daniel considered the question for a moment. "Student life was very different to anything I'd experienced before. In my second year, I met someone, but that didn't work out." A deep crease furrowed his brow but vanished as quickly as it had appeared. "It was fun living in a student house, and I made some good friends. Then I graduated."

We carried on walking, passing the locked gate to the botanical gardens.

"So, what did you do afterwards?" I prompted, hoping he would carry on confiding in me.

"I went back home, intending to stay with Mum for only a few weeks, but she had changed — she'd stopped living. Seeing her pretending at daily life, I knew I had to put my future on hold. I spent the next eighteen months helping her through depression. I took on bar work and a part-time job in a warehouse to pay for her therapy. Eventually, her drinking stopped, and the professional help was working."

"So, things were starting to look up for you both?"

The path we were ambling along bent around a copse of trees, behind which was a shallow duck pond with benches scattered around its perimeter. I gestured for Daniel to sit. He folded himself down elegantly onto the curved green metal bench.

"Yeah," he continued. "Mum had a new job and was pleased to have a reason to start each day again. That summer, some uni friends invited me to join them across Europe. The idea was that we would work to pay our way as we backpacked from country to country. I was worried to leave Mum in case she relapsed, but she insisted I go." He turned to me, his eyes bright. "Christopher, it was amazing, the things we did. I picked fruit in Spain, washed hospital laundry in Germany and slept under the stars on a beach in southern Italy. The year was wild with work and parties. I phoned Mum whenever I could, and she always sounded like she was doing well. She had even started dating a 'wonderful man' and couldn't be happier.

"At first, Andy seemed harmless," Daniel said, his gaze fixed on a duck that drifted slowly across the surface of the pond. "But I remember the day I met him. He made me really nervous."

Daniel's left knee started to bounce up and down with restless energy. He was oblivious to its movement.

"We hated each other instantly. While I was away, Mum's relationship with Andy had grown intense, and he had moved in. I saw through him, but Mum couldn't do enough and tended to his every need. Of course she was loving the attention he gave her.

"When I first got back, I found evening work in a local bar," Daniel said. "But Mum had cut the number of hours she worked each week because Andy wanted her to stay at home more. Because of my own work, I only had a few hours alone with her each week. Anyway, one day I noticed a bruise on her arm."

"Oh no..." I leaned forward on the bench.

"Yep. And when I asked how she got it, she made up some rubbish story, but I gave her the benefit of the doubt. A week later, she was in hospital. Andy said she had fallen down the stairs, but I don't think that explained the black eye. I confronted her and said I wasn't stupid. She denied anything bad had happened and said it was just an accident. When I asked Andy about it, he slammed me against a wall and put his hand around my throat. He made it clear that if I wasn't out of the flat in twenty-four hours, I would end up in hospital, too."

Daniel stood abruptly. "Do you mind if we walk some more?"

"No," I answered, jumping up. We had completed a loop of the park and were now heading back in the direction of the flat. We walked on in silence, and I was just thinking that Daniel wasn't going to carry on with his story when he suddenly spoke.

"So, with the help of a friend, I took my few belongings to my aunt's home in Shropshire, then went down to London with just a rucksack of essentials. Aunt Liz was due to be moving to Bristol in a matter of weeks, so I stayed in London, calling in favours from mates, sleeping on sofas, taking on temp work. I thought I could go to Bristol when she moved. I didn't want to stay in Shropshire, even though she offered. I wanted to be near my mates and better work opportunities. Anyway, when we met on the train, I was headed to Bristol, thinking I'd ring Aunt Liz when I was there. She didn't have a number for me, see? Turns out her move had been delayed, and she was still in bloody Shropshire. Anyway, I stayed with a friend in Bristol, but last week I was tipped off about work at the restaurant in Bath. So I thought it would be easier to stay at the YMCA here. But then today happened… So all my worldly belongings are currently in an attic in Shropshire, and I'm wearing someone else's underwear."

Daniel turned to me and offered a resigned grin. I was at a complete loss about what to say. Some people would have given up, but Daniel was clearly following a path. Unpleasant things had happened, yet he could shake them off, pick himself up and move on. He somehow knew where he was meant to be. I wished I had known him sooner.

We arrived back at the flat and went through to the lounge. I thought about asking him to stay another night, then I thought about Oliver. There were some things that were still not clear to me.

"Have you heard from Oliver?" I asked casually, rearranging the cushions on the sofa that were fine as they were.

Daniel was standing in front of my father's pictures once more. He turned to me and shook his head. "He wanted to give me his mobile number, but I said I didn't have a phone. Too expensive."

"Oh," I replied. "I just wondered. You and Oliver, you met at a gay bar, are you two...?"

"Oh God no!" Daniel exclaimed. "I'd only been in Bath a couple of days and didn't fancy spending the evening alone, so I went to a pub. He bought me a few drinks and invited me back to his. I knew what he wanted, but I wasn't leading him on, either. In fact, I didn't even know I was in a gay pub."

"Ah, okay..." I could tell by the surprise and distaste on Daniel's face that what he was saying was the truth.

"To be honest, I felt bad about knocking back his advances."

"Don't be," I assured him. "That arrogance he has is a dangerous thing. He thinks he can have whatever he wants. He is weirdly wonderful, but he also has a very short attention span."

Daniel nodded. "Yeah, he caught me off guard. I shouldn't have gone back to his. I'm not interested in him in that way. It was just nice to have someone to talk to. That's why I asked to meet at the pub the next day." Daniel cast his eyes down at the floor. "He's the only person I know in Bath," he added.

"Well, you know me as well now," I offered, heartened that he looked back up at me gratefully.

He held my gaze for a second and smiled. "Perhaps I shouldn't have told him where I work. He came into the restaurant last night wanting to see me. He was extremely rude to the manager when he was told I was busy working. When I found out, of course I was mortified and apologised. I don't want to lose my job because of him."

I winced, picturing the scene. "Unfortunately, Oliver doesn't understand the word 'no'."

It reminded me of a time when he and I met for dinner one evening a couple of years ago. I chose the restaurant, a small Italian bistro that was one of my favourites in the city. We'd only been seated at our table a short while. The smiling young waitress brought over a basket of bread and a jug of water. I poured us each a glass as we perused the menu.

"This is bloody tepid," he said, after taking a sip. "Excuse me, yes, you."

The waitress looked around at our table, her eyes wide. Other diner's conversations had frozen mid-sentence, disturbed by the volume of his voice.

"Is it really too much to expect some bloody ice and a few slices of lemon in this?" He picked up the jug and brandished it at her. "If you can't even get the table water right, what the hell is the food going to be like?"

I looked away as he laughed, watching her retreating figure as she scurried off towards the kitchen. A few minutes later, a male waiter returned bearing another jug of water, ice clinking within and beads of condensation running down the sides.

"Here you go, gentlemen. I'll come back and take your order in one moment."

Oliver looked puzzled. "Where's the waitress gone?"

"She's busy with other duties at the moment."

"Too scared to serve us, you mean. I bet she's having a good old cry out the back by the bins." Oliver laughed again, and I heard the scorn in it.

"Sir, if I could ask you to keep your voice down. The other diners…"

Oliver sat back in his chair and stared at the waiter. I picked up the menu and studied it intently, dreading the inevitable.

"I come in here, happy to pay good money to eat your food, and now you're telling me to keep my voice down? How dare you!" he roared. Oliver pushed the bread basket aside, sending slices of baguette skittering across the table. He stood up, shunting his chair back behind him, the legs screeching against the tiled floor.

"Let's find somewhere else to eat, Chris. I've lost my appetite for Italian food."

My lasting memory of that restaurant was of myself mumbling apologies to diners and waiting staff alike as I meekly followed in Oliver's stormy wake. I had never plucked up the courage to go back.

I dismissed the memory, not wanting to share it with Daniel. He should make up his own mind about Oliver. I didn't want to tell tales or talk negatively about him behind his back.

"So, do you live here alone? Pretty nice place you've got."

"Yes, I'm by myself. What about you?"

He flinched a little. "Yes, I've been single since uni. Since *Hector*."

He rolled the syllables around as he said the name.

"Hector?" I asked.

"Yes," Daniel said. "Doesn't suit a young person, does it? It's more apt for someone with elbow patches on their jacket."

I was elated Daniel's relationship was with another man, but that made me think about how desperately Oliver wanted to know if Daniel was gay or not.

"How did you meet?" I asked.

"Well…I was pretty lost in my first year at uni, to be honest. I didn't want to go out with other students and drink every night. I kind of knew I was gay, but I wasn't ready to tell anyone yet. There was no one I trusted. I even went out on a couple of dates with girls."

"Took me a while, too," I said.

"Things got better in my second year when I moved into a shared house. We all got on, and a couple of months later, I even went to the LGBT society on campus. Well, I bottled out a couple of times and hung around outside for a while. That was when Hector appeared. He asked if I was coming in. I replied that actually I was coming out, which he thought was funny.

"He looked after me all evening, and when we left, he asked if I wanted to go for a drink. We just went to the student union bar but hit it off pretty much straight away. He was funny, charming and a bit geeky. We started seeing each other, and things were good for a few weeks, until I met his friend Josh. This guy was physically imposing. Whenever they were together, they were as thick as thieves. I thought it strange that a nerdy history student and a gym instructor were best friends, as if there was something going on between them that blurred the lines, you know? Anyway, Josh hated me from the start. Mostly he would ignore me, but sometimes he was just hostile. Hector didn't want to hear about it, but I rarely got to see him by himself anyway, as he was always with Josh and I just joined them, down at the pub. It was a bizarre threesome, where both Josh and I vied for Hector's attention. This went on for about a few months, but then something happened the weekend before we were supposed to break for Easter…"

He turned pale and wrung his hands.

"You don't have to tell me…"

"No, it's fine. I need to say it. I've never said it out loud to anybody before. Can I trust you?"

I nodded as a wave of nausea rushed through my guts.

"We drank a lot that night," he said. "Josh was just being his usual bastard self, and I had to stop myself from snapping at him. Anyway, Hector decided we should carry on drinking back at mine after the pub had shut. They knew my housemates had already gone home for the holidays, so I couldn't say no. They hated Josh as much as I did, to be honest. Josh went to the off-licence, and I went back to my student digs with Hector, leaving the door on the latch for Josh. But as soon as we got in, Hector started touching me. He was really drunk and horny. I was drunk, too, and we kissed a bit, but I could tell he wanted more. I was still a virgin, and I knew that frustrated him."

Daniel's hands were now starting to shake a little. Ptolemy came into the room and curled around his legs.

"You don't have to tell me..." I repeated, and Ptolemy mewed, as if to confirm this.

"No, I'm okay. So, Hector pushed me down on the sofa and started groping me anyway. Then Josh came in, and I told Hector to stop, but instead, Josh asked him if he needed any help. I started to struggle, but Josh came over and pinned me down. He was so fucking strong. Hector was so drunk. He just pulled my jeans off."

"Oh my God..."

"I reckon Hector was in love with Josh, but Josh wasn't into guys. In fact, he was shagging his way 'round campus, including several girls I knew. But he still wanted to control Hector, and that included controlling me. Anyhow, Hector took off my T-shirt and used it to cover my face. I couldn't breathe. I thought I was going to die. Then Josh was just yelling encouragement, as Hector did what he wanted to me. I've never told a soul."

Daniel's face crumpled, and he sobbed. "That Easter, I didn't know if I could carry on. I was in a very dark place. I almost didn't go back. But then I thought about how proud my mum was that I was doing my degree. When I saw Hector the next term, he said it was a bit of drunken fun and claimed he couldn't remember much anyway. But at the same time, I could tell he was terrified."

"And you had to see him around most days?"

"I just pretended he didn't exist."

"You really are one of the strongest people I've met, Daniel."

"Well, it doesn't always feel like that."

* * * *

That evening we ate a big meal at the dining table, washed up together and finished off the evening by sharing more wine. I listened to stories about his travels and also told him about how I had lost my parents. Just before midnight, I took the extra blanket off my bed and gave it to Daniel. I wanted to make the sofa comfortable for him.

"Thank you for letting me stay another night. I promise I'll be out of your hair by tomorrow."

I didn't want him to leave. I cleaned my teeth then went into the bedroom where Ptolemy was waiting for me on the bed. I undressed, turned off the light and climbed beneath the duvet, feeling the cold from the lack of the extra layer. In the darkness I placed my hands behind my head and hoped that, once I fell asleep, the answers would appear in my dreams.

Chapter Seven

Something that did not belong to me was shimmering next to the tap on the bathroom sink. It was a ring. Up close, it was exquisite. It had that soft dull gleam which only emanated from gold. It was designed with intricate connected leaves woven into a circle, which reminded me of the laurel wreaths worn on the heads of gods in Greek mythology. I pushed open the lounge door, Ptolemy at my heels. The morning light seeped through the edges of the blinds, illuminating the room with soft shadows. Daniel was buried deep in the blanket, his body swaddled, only his head and bare shoulders to be seen. He shifted when he realised somebody was in the room.

"Morning," he murmured, rubbing his eyes.

"How are you feeling?"

"I haven't slept like that in ages," he replied.

I pulled up the blinds to let the world back in. It was still early, but people were up and about and on their way to work. The sky was pale grey, with clouds thick enough to make sure no real sunlight would penetrate through them much today, but I didn't mind. As I made breakfast, the sound of water hammered through the flat while Daniel took a shower. I carried everything through to the lounge and noticed how neatly he had folded his bedding. I poured fresh orange juice into tumblers, and by the time Daniel had finished his shower, I had created a grand breakfast.

"Oh wow!"

"It's just a bit of toast..." I said, turning the radio on.

He pulled out a chair and sat at the table. I remembered the ring and delved into my pocket to retrieve it.

"I found this by the bathroom sink," I said.

"Oh, yes..."

"It looks expensive."

"It is," he said, taking it from me. "Who do you think would give me a ring and at the same time tell me its value?"

I laughed.

"Oliver gave it to me on Sunday after we dropped you off here. I didn't know what to do. For a minute, I thought he was going to propose."

"It seems he has a thing for you, then."

"I've only met him twice. It's a bit much, don't you think?"

"It's pretty typical of Oliver to carry out such a grand gesture while also turning it into a vulgar display of affluence after only knowing someone for five minutes."

"I'll take your word for it. Do you have his address? I need to post this vulgar thing back. If it is as expensive as he said, I don't want to be carrying it around for too long, especially at the YMCA."

I knew he was waiting until the end of the week to get paid. He could have easily sold the ring and Oliver would have been none the wiser.

"Oh, you're going back?"

"Well, yes, I have no choice. I should see if my stuff's turned up, anyway."

"Okay, but look, just borrow this, so you can get some clothes," I reached into my wallet and pulled out some banknotes.

"I cannot accept those."

"Yes, you can. Pay me back when you get paid."

"Christopher, I can't —"

"No arguments. We need to get going, otherwise I'm going to be late for work."

We walked along the path behind the flat. From above, we could have been one of those couples I often gazed upon. Maybe a neighbour was looking down right now thinking about us. Daniel walked close to me, his arm occasionally brushing against mine, sending a thrill through me. Was it lust? Or excitement? Being this close to him released butterflies in my stomach. I was worried our time together was almost at an end. I wanted him to be by my side forever. I imagined walking into a pub or a party with him on my arm, the pride I would feel as people looked at us…the perfect couple. I wanted them to see that yes, I could love, and yes, I was loved. I wanted to shout it from the rooftops.

"I could buy you a drink after my shift today?" he said. "I know it doesn't match what you've done for me, but it's all I've got right now. I want to say thanks for letting me stay."

I went to work on a high, having agreed to meet later outside the restaurant when Daniel finished. Throughout the day, my mind was occupied with the conundrum that was Daniel. There was no doubt he was having a bad time, but what made me feel sad was that he seemed so alone. He had mentioned the favours of friends, but he had never mentioned anyone by name. Meanwhile, his father was nowhere. He could have gone to Oliver but hadn't. By returning the ring, he clearly intended to halt any advances. The thought of how to proceed, or even making a gameplan, seemed sneaky and self-profiting, so I gave up imagining scenarios and decided all he needed was someone to be a real friend. It wasn't about me anymore.

I pressed on with the day and immersed myself in the books around me. Since starting at the bookshop, my knowledge had increased a thousandfold. Subjects I had previously known nothing about now sparked all sorts of curiosity within me. Thinking back to the less enlightened version of myself, I imagined I was like Paul with the scales falling from his eyes after being blinded on the road to Damascus. The clock ticked away, and it wasn't long before it was time to close the shop and meet Daniel.

I was starting to get nervous. I ran a broom over the floor, the ritual calming me down. When Art first had the shop, the floors had been covered with cheap lino, but as he had renovated, he had discovered antique parquet flooring underneath. He had restored the wood, so the warm glow radiating from it complemented the book-lined rooms. I enjoyed being in the shop alone. I always pretended it was my own private library. I breathed in deeply, savouring the unmistakable smell that all bookshops had.

I was careful not to arrive at the restaurant too early. I killed time by peering into shop fronts, looking at the displays. Our window display was Tabitha's domain, and she often went to town with creations that hung from wires or emerged from artificial landscapes. Passersby were constantly stopping to look.

When I reached the restaurant, I stayed a respectful distance from the window, as I didn't want to be caught peering in while people were eating. I could make out the bar and the copper-domed lamps that hung low, projecting light along the stainless-steel surface. Shelves of glasses sparkled on the wall behind. Daniel was standing by a table, performing the pantomime of opening a bottle of wine and offering the first sip for approval. He looked smart and professional, the cut of his black trousers contoured his lower body perfectly, contrasting with his white open-necked shirt. He glanced up towards the window, startling me. Had he perceived me as a voyeur? He subtly waved and indicated with his fingers that he would be a couple of minutes.

I stepped over the cobbles to look into the shop next door. Great wheels of cheese lay entombed in wax, leaning against each other like forgotten tyres in a dusty old garage. My stomach rumbled. Daniel was now heading towards me with a new rucksack on his shoulder and several shopping bags in each hand. As we walked to a nearby pub, he told me about his day.

"I spent two hours trying to find clothes for work. Hopefully I can fit everything in the rucksack. The YMCA said they looked at their camera footage but couldn't see anyone leaving with my stuff. When I go back this evening, I'll pay a bit extra for a private room. It should be more secure."

"You're going back, then?" I said, the disappointment evident in my voice.

"Well, I don't have a choice."

"Stay at mine," I said on impulse.

"What? No, you've been too good already. I'll be fine," he replied dismissively.

"I mean it. Stay at mine. Stay on the sofa, and save some cash. You can put it towards a rent deposit for somewhere else."

"Thanks, but..." Daniel's steps faltered, and he glanced at me. I could see the uncertainty on his face.

"Look. It's nice having someone around, and your stuff will be safe." It felt pushy, so I left the offer dangling.

We had reached the pub, and I went to the window table with his bags as he went to the bar. He came back with two pints and set them down.

"Are you sure about letting me stay?"

I nodded, relieved that I hadn't come across as too keen.

"I merely intended to say thanks by buying you a pint, and now you're being even more generous."

Had I been too quick? Could it work, two people living in a one-bedroom flat? Would he want to stay? It wouldn't be for long.

"It's no problem."

"While I appreciate it, it doesn't seem fair. Would I be in the way?"

"I wouldn't have offered if I didn't mean it. Because of work, we wouldn't even see each other half the time, anyway."

"True," he conceded. "I guess I could stay for a few days and get myself sorted. I won't outstay my welcome. Thank you. Again."

By the time we left the pub, it was considerably colder than when we had arrived. We walked back, our faces falling forward into our coat collars to protect from the chill. Fifteen minutes later, we were back at the flat ordering pizza. It seemed surreal but also natural. Daniel was sorting his new clothes and folding them neatly in his new rucksack, while Oliver's ring lay on the coffee table nearby. I was impressed at how he could fit everything he needed in a single rucksack. I thought of him being well-practiced after travelling.

"Here," I said, placing a key on the table next to the ring. "This is for you, so you can come and go as you please."

"Oh, okay. Thanks."

We spent the next few days performing a polite and delicate ballet with each other. I wanted to stop him worrying about getting in my way, but like a kitten on its first time in a new home, he never strayed far from the sofa.

Those first days passed in a blur, with both of us working. I told him there was no need for him to leave the flat at the same time as I did, that he was fine to stay there alone. The next morning, I went into the lounge shortly after he had left for work. I felt unsettled. There was something different about the room.

The photo of the paddle steamer was missing. I had been sure the picture was there the night before. I left for work, keen not to assume the worst, but I spent the day unable to stop thinking about it. By five p.m., in readiness for confrontation, I had a speech rehearsed. As I approached my front door, I grew nervous. I turned the key and quietly let myself in. Maybe I would catch him in the act of something else. I passed the chest of drawers in the hallway and saw there was now another picture next to the portrait of my parents. I went into the lounge to find Daniel reading on the sofa and the paddle steamer back on the wall.

"You framed the picture of Ptolemy?"

I had kept a photo of a much-younger Ptolemy on my bookshelf. I had been meaning to get it framed for quite some time.

"I hope you don't mind. I know how much you love that picture and thought it was a shame that it wasn't framed. I borrowed one of your other pictures to match the wood."

He turned back to his book, and I went out to the hallway to stand in front of the pictures, a gentle reminder of what it was to be happy.

Chapter Eight

It was early morning. Outside, the city was quiet. I normally didn't mind working at the weekend, but today I was sad to be away from Daniel. He had now been with me in the flat for almost two weeks. It was typical that he had the Saturday off and would be working all afternoon and evening Sunday. I spent the day wondering what Daniel was doing. Was he reading or looking for somewhere else to live? I missed the ritual of Sunday roast and wondered if it was something he had also enjoyed when he was growing up. With his father gone and his mother's money problems, I doubted it. I made a note to cook roast beef for him when he had a Sunday off, if he hadn't found anywhere else to live by then.

I grabbed groceries on my way home, then headed back to the flat, my feet aching from the day spent on my feet. I walked in to find Daniel in the hallway dressed for work. He even had his apron on.

"Oh, I didn't know you were working today?"

"I am, but not at the restaurant. May I take your coat?"

I handed it over, and he hung it up.

"This way, sir," he said, indicating towards the lounge.

There were several tea-lights dotted around, the room lit by their wavering glow. The blinds were pulled tight, with only a sliver of light shining through. He had moved the table so that it was now beneath the photos. It was the perfect backdrop. The pictures came alive as shadows from the candlelight danced among them. Quiet music drifted across the room. Cutlery and glasses gleamed on top of a light-grey linen tablecloth and napkins that did not belong to me. Small plates laden with appetisers graced the coffee table. An opened bottle of red wine waited, its contents breathing. I had been holding my breath since I'd walked into the room, and I now exhaled.

"What's going on?" I asked.

He pulled out a chair at the table and waited behind it. I sat and watched as he glided through the ritual of serving me.

"It's not my birthday," I continued. "Or have you broken something?"

He took off his apron, sat opposite me and raised a glass. I touched my glass to his, the chime resonating briefly in the air.

"Sorry. That whole performance was ridiculous, but I did say I'd cook for you. There's antipasti to start with, then lasagne and lemon syllabub."

"It's great. Truly. But you should be saving your cash."

"It's all good. You won't take any money from me for letting me stay, so…"

He had brought up the subject of money the day before, too. I could tell he was frustrated at not being able to pay his way.

"I got a few things from the restaurant, and they let me have some ingredients, too. Plus, I swung by that deli that you like." He fetched a plate from the coffee table, and I pointed towards a stubby, almost-black tube on the platter.

"What on earth is that?"

"That's *butifarra embutido*, otherwise known as sausage. From Spain."

I laughed. His comment dissipated any worries I had about not being such a connoisseur. I then tried *casunziei* ravioli filled with chopped beets, roasted Greek fennel bulb sautéed in garlic and Polish *sledzie* herring, which lay on a bed of sliced onion with an oily marinade. It delicately fell apart as it touched my tongue. We then had artichoke, the ash still on its outer leaves from the embers of the fire it had been cooked in, a smoky tender heart hidden at the centre. Daniel went into the kitchen to put finishing touches on the lasagne.

"Where did you learn to cook?" I asked as he came back into the room, two plates on one arm and a rustic green salad on the other.

"At uni. My housemates were just eating pasta and supermarket sauce. I wanted nicer food, so I bought cookbooks and experimented. The rest I picked up from working in bars and restaurants. You get to know about wine, too, if you work in one of the more upmarket places. It was the travelling that really opened me up to great food, though. I ate freshly caught fish with my fingers in Greece. It had just been cooked on the harbourside, and it only had a dash of olive oil and a squeeze of lemon added. It was amazing."

"Ever considered becoming a chef?"

"Maybe one day. I just need to get myself sorted here first."

Feeling grounded and permanent in Bath was important to me, but it was clear this wasn't the case for Daniel. He was a free spirit who could move or settle anywhere. Just because he was here now didn't mean he always would be. I admired and envied the way he headed into the unknown. Everything I knew came from books — everything he knew came from living. That was the difference between us. I hid from the world, and he embraced it.

He left the room and reappeared cradling the lasagne. The smell was incredible, a hint of red wine and oregano coming through the delicious mix of beef, onion and garlic. We ate, talked and drank, but all the while I was luxuriating in the moment and the thrill of the effort he had gone to. The way he had transformed the lounge into a restaurant, the little touches with the candles and tablecloth. And how incredible he looked too, with his ironed shirt showing off the contours of his upper frame, the top two buttons undone to reveal a glimpse of his collarbone. I had to quell the urge to trace the outline with my finger, so I focused on the flawlessness of his face. The candle flames danced and reflected in his eyes, mirroring his hands as he talked about dessert.

"I didn't make these," he confessed. "They're from the restaurant, and they're insanely bad for your health."

I savoured the sweet creamy texture of the syllabub, before the sharp prick of fresh lemon zest revealed itself. He watched as I enjoyed every mouthful, but I didn't know what he was thinking. I normally never ate sweet things, but I was enjoying his gaze. I glanced up to meet his eyes but feared it was for a second too long.

He looked away and said, "Oliver's up on Lansdown, isn't he? I still need his address."

I felt as if a spell had been broken. "He does. It's up a pretty steep hill, though."

"Oh yes, I remember now. I'll walk up in the morning and post the ring through his letterbox."

I pictured the scene, Oliver opening the door to catch Daniel in the act, with envelope in hand. I then imagined Daniel going into the apartment, and the door closing, shutting me out of the frame. I almost offered to post the envelope on Daniel's behalf, but decided it was best not to get involved. Later, after dinner, I saw him scribbling a note, which he put it in the envelope with the ring before sealing it down with tape. I was desperate to know what he had written. He didn't dwell on it and instead opened up the conversation to my favourite subject – a diversionary tactic, I was sure. "Your books," he said. "It all seems very… organised."

I laughed and pointed to a low shelf. "Yes, maybe. These books here are what I'm currently reading, and…" I turned to the other bookshelves. "The rest are filed by category. So over there I have books on music, here I keep all my fiction, there I have some books on art and travel and these shelves right here hold my collection of gay literature."

He took a seat on the sofa. I picked out a book and sat next to him. "This is the first book I read that had a gay storyline," I said.

He read the title out loud in a slow and considered way, before asking, "Can I read it?"

"Sure. Would you like another one, too?"

He nodded and said, "Pick one for me."

I sensed something flirtatious about his manner. Reluctant to leave his side, I turned back to the shelves and ran my finger along the spines then selected *The Swimming-Pool Library*. "A modern-day gay classic. See what you think."

Chapter Nine

Not only had Daniel walked to Oliver's to post the ring back, but he had also made arrangements to look at some rented rooms. This made me anxious. He promised he would be out of my hair as soon as possible. I didn't see him much early in the week, and on his one night off, I had been invited to dinner by an old friend called Graham. I walked to the southeast of the city where Graham lived. It was balmy, so we stayed outside among the trees in the garden, the branches casting shadows in the evening sun.

Over gin and tonics, we reminisced about school, as we always did when we caught up, but I was distracted. From the garden, I could see the Royal Crescent as well as the row of rooftops where my flat was. I imagined Daniel circling more rooms for rent in the local paper, cursing at how uncomfortable my sofa was. At the end of the evening, I walked back to the flat, taking in the lights of the homes that I passed, grabbing snapshots of domestic life through the slashes of curtains that hadn't been quite pulled together. Moving from room to room, everyone looked content, watching television, drinking wine. I remembered what life was like living together as a family, but I had no experience of living with a partner. Sharing waking moments with each other… The good and the bad… Creating an unbreakable bond… Loving and comforting each other… These all seemed such a natural thing to do. I craved it like an old addiction.

I was glad to be walking home. It would take a while, and it would give me time to think about the evening. I had told Graham about Daniel and was surprised when he didn't seem as happy for me as I was expecting. I told him a little about Daniel's history, and he sympathised, but he had also raised the idea that I was being played and that I should be careful. He thought it strange that Daniel would seek out the help of a complete stranger, then ingratiate himself into my life by taking advantage of my good nature.

"Why didn't he just stay with his aunt until she was ready to move to Bristol? Saying he wanted to be near his mates and then sofa-surfing sounds a bit weird to me, especially when he's got a perfectly good place with his aunt," he reasoned. I didn't have an answer. I knew Graham had my best interests at heart. He had known me since I was eleven, and he was always candid. He tactfully listed some of my attempted relationships, making my track record sound weak. He also pointed out I needed someone stable who lived locally, not a homeless stranger who was just passing through. I mulled over our conversation for the rest of the journey home. I was angry and worried.

When I awoke the next morning, Daniel had already left. I assumed he had more rooms to view before work.

I went through to the lounge, taking in the scent of him as I plumped the cushions on the sofa. He returned later that evening to a clean house and fresh laundry.

"How was your day?" I asked.

He eyed up a shirt I had ironed for him.

"Long," he said. "Mind if I grab a beer?"

He seemed agitated, so I hesitated, not quite wanting to ask the question, but desperate to know the answer.

"How did it go?" I asked.

He raised his eyebrows.

"The rented rooms. You went to see some?"

"Oh, yeah. I saw four places in all..."

"And?"

"One was filthy and on the outskirts, so it was quite a trek. I couldn't wait to get out of there."

He grimaced before continuing, "Two were okay, and the other people renting were nice enough. The fourth room was perfect, as it's twenty minutes from work and there's only one other person living there."

"So...?"

"I still need to save for the deposit, which is more than I earn in a month right now." He banged the beer down on the table.

"Let's talk about it over dinner. Stay there."

I brought out a pile of fresh *tagliatelle verde*, stuffed chicken breasts and roasted vegetables. It was colourful, if nothing else.

"Wow, that looks good," said Daniel.

"So, what are your options then?"

"I can either go back to the YMCA or move back to Bristol where it's cheaper. I like the job in Bath, so I could get the bus in."

"All you're doing right now is flitting from place to place. When does your aunt move to Bristol? It can't be that long now?" I thought about the conversation with Graham the evening before.

"Another couple of months," he said with a worried look.

"If you rented, you might have to commit for longer than that."

Despite anything Graham thought, I was pleased I had quickly come up with a reason why renting might not be such a good idea for Daniel. All I needed was for him to realise that living with me wasn't an inconvenience. He rubbed his chin, looking embarrassed. "Yeah, I know. If that happened, I was hoping I could find someone to move in and take over my contract. I can't go back to my friend's sofa in Bristol, because she's moving out soon. I phoned her."

"You could just stay here, you know, Daniel."

"I can't take advantage of you any longer."

Part of me felt selfish wanting him to stay. I knew it benefited him financially, but having his company and proximity was worth so much more to me. I enjoyed talking to him, cooking for him. I found myself thinking I could get used to this. I was not about to start pleading, but he seemed indecisive.

"Having you here has made me realise I don't want to be alone anymore."

Deep crimson spread across his cheeks and neck. I waited.

"I promise I won't get in the way," he said eventually.

* * * *

We settled into a comfortable rhythm of living together. Daniel relaxed and insisted on buying food for us both to enjoy. Apart from the evenings when he had to work, dinner became a ritual. We planned meals and delegated tasks. Like a play, there were two acts, the creation and the consumption. We enjoyed cooking in my tiny kitchen, then, with all the finesse of a posh restaurant, we sat at a table adorned with napkins and a tablecloth, telling each other about our days. April soon became May, and we fell into another routine as the evenings became warmer and lighter. After dinner, we walked in the park, ambling along the pebbled paths, treading over the blossoms that littered the ground, the petals muddied and bruised. We talked about everything and nothing or stayed comfortable together in silence. At the flat, we read until it was time to sleep. Daniel was now devouring a steady stream of recommendations. He couldn't read fast enough.

This evening, Daniel was working. His shift had finished at ten, and I was expecting him back at any minute. I had already poured him a glass of wine. Ptolemy snoozed, his eyes half closed, a rumble of contentment emerging as I absently stroked his fur. The key turned in the lock. It was now a sound that triggered a warm response in me, making me giddy and excited. Daniel came into the flat and stood at the doorway of the sitting room. He looked tired and handsome.

"Mind if I take a quick shower before we eat?" he asked.

"Of course not. There's wine here waiting when you're ready."

I lay back on the sofa and continued with my book, letting the sound of the shower wash over me as if I was in there with Daniel, too. Just as I finished the chapter, a succession of knocks sounded on the front door. They continued, not frantically, but with some impatience. I went out to the hallway, glancing at the photos of my parents and Ptolemy as I passed through. I opened the door to find Oliver standing on the other side, his hand raised mid-knock. He glared at me in an unfocused way, and I realised he was drunk.

"Oliver. It's getting late."

"Sorry. I was just passing and one of your neighbours was leaving, so I thought I'd come up. And here I am, you see."

He grinned and opened his arms wide, expecting a hug. A bottle of wine swung from his left hand.

"I was just about to go to bed. I have work tomorrow. Can we meet in the week? In fact, I've been meaning to call..."

He dropped his arms, and they swung loosely at his sides. "Why is everyone so fucking *boring*?" he announced. "C'mon, Chris. Let's have a drink, then go out somewhere. I want to get wasted."

He laughed uproariously, and at that moment, Daniel emerged from the bathroom. I closed my eyes, knowing this moment was long overdue. All three actors had been called to the stage. I turned. Daniel was standing outside the bathroom door, barefoot, wearing only black jeans. There was a look of panic on his face. I gazed at his naked torso, and in that one brief second, a heady rush of lust overtook me.

"What the fuck?" Oliver said, his voice monotone. There was a moment of silence, and nobody moved.

"It's not what you think," I said, closing the door slightly on him. His gaze shifted over to me.

"What *am* I supposed to think then? Could it be you've taken what's rightfully mine?"

"Hey, I don't belong to anybody," said Daniel indignantly.

"You fucking snake," Oliver said.

"Don't speak to Daniel like that. Otherwise, I'll—"

"Or what? What are you going to do?" His voice grew in intensity. He narrowed in on Daniel. "First you return the ring I got you. Wasn't it expensive enough for you? Then you run 'round here and jump into bed with him. You're a fucking whore!"

Daniel flinched as if he had been physically struck.

"For fuck's sake, Oliver," I shouted, "you can't just turn up here and throw insults. Nothing has happened. Daniel has been sleeping on the sofa. I'm helping him out. And he is not your property."

Oliver hurled the bottle of wine through the door.

"Oh my God!" Daniel shouted.

The bottle crashed into the chest of drawers and exploded, knocking the two picture frames to the ground. Wine ran down the walls and pooled onto the floor among the shards of glass. Daniel looked at me in shock.

"What the fuck?" I said to Oliver. He stood back in the doorway, then turned to run down the stairs. We heard the main door slam.

"Jesus. Are you okay?" I said to Daniel.

"I'm so sorry," he said. His hands were shaking. "This is my fault. I can't stay here if this is what's going to happen. Let me clean this up and then I'll pack my things."

"You are not going anywhere. This isn't your fault. Oliver's mad. He made up his own mind about what he saw. You did the decent thing and returned the ring.

He just couldn't stand the thought of you refusing him. Let's clean this mess up."

The picture frames were undamaged, but the glass was cracked. I wiped down the walls, and we blotted up the wine from the floor and swept the glass.

"What a waste of alcohol," Daniel said. I laughed. The relief of it felt good.

It was nearly midnight by the time we were ready for bed. I said goodnight and closed my bedroom door. It took a while to fall asleep, as I was still reeling. A couple of hours later, I awoke with a start. I thought I had heard a noise. Then I heard it again, a tentative knock at my bedroom door.

"Daniel?"

The door opened, and I could just make him out standing there, silhouetted in the soft hallway light. He was clad just in his undershorts. "I don't want to be alone anymore, either," he said.

I moved to the side of the bed and threw back the duvet on the empty half of the mattress, and he walked towards the bed. The world held its breath, allowing us to be the only ones who existed in that moment, a singular point in time where nothing else mattered.

Chapter Ten

Will, another old school friend of mine and Graham's, was getting married and had asked us to the wedding. I wanted Daniel to come with me but decided to wait and see how things went between us before I asked him. However, when I accepted the invitation, I had forgotten I would be expected to attend the stag do as well. Will had caught me unawares, and I wasn't able to come up with an excuse as to why I couldn't attend the party in Bristol, which he assured me would be a "riotous affair". Who was I kidding, though? It wasn't as if my diary was brimming with social events. As for the plus-one guest to the wedding, who would want to suffer the boredom of a day spent offering platitudes to strangers, while standing around watching the photographer trying to round up children and in-laws for a group photo? All that in exchange for a free meal and some passable wine. At least if I had Daniel by my side, it would be more bearable.

Will and I had been better friends when we were teenagers and caught up every once in a while just to dust off the cobwebs of our friendship and remind ourselves of more carefree times. Graham had already said he couldn't make it, as his wife was due to give birth. The idea of a stag do filled me with dread. The drunken and shambling carnage of a stag or hen party on the streets of Bath, the pack mentality of a group of inebriated men reduced to the status of lumbering Neanderthals... These things scared me. What intimidated me the most, though, was the threat that these people could, at any moment, fall into violence.

I just wanted to stay home, but Daniel persuaded me it would be all right and that I would have a good time. I did wonder if he was waiting for me to invite him to the wedding. As such, I didn't go on too much about how stag dos were almost a phobia of mine. I should have said no, but I had committed to it now and parted with some cash, too. I had never been on one before, but thought I should get over my fear, so I ended up saying yes — something I instantly regretted.

Simon, Will's best man, phoned me to share the details of the testosterone-fuelled day. We were due to meet in a pub in Bristol at eleven in the morning the following week. As much as my social life involved drinking, I knew that even the promise of alcohol wouldn't help me out much, especially at that hour. I hoped to get away early. I just wanted to be with Daniel and could feel the longing like an ache throughout my body.

The train pulled into Bristol Temple Meads railway station with a drawn-out squeal. I disembarked, joining the morning shoppers, envious that their days would probably be more enjoyable than mine.

There was a group of men standing outside the pub talking to a barmaid as she opened the front doors.

They went in, and as I followed behind, I gave her a little smile. I didn't want her to think I was like them. The pub was a clone of all the others up and down the land. I felt some temporary relief when I saw Will.

"Chris! You made it! Let's get you a beer."

Within moments I had a drink in my hand and was being introduced to the group. Will had invited some colleagues, along with Simon, another childhood friend. And there was someone else, too.

"You must remember Rory from school?" Will said to me.

Rory was wearing sunglasses indoors, something that always made me dislike people. Even though he was part of the group of friends I used to hang around with, we had never liked each other. He always had something cruel to say, but I never rose to the bait, not wanting him to know how much he annoyed me. And now, I still wanted to be the better man. I put my hand out, and he removed his sunglasses before squeezing my fingers together a little too tightly. I made sure not to react as I met his gaze.

"Rory, it's been a while."

He studied my face, scanning for discomfort as he gripped harder. After realising he wasn't going to get a reaction, he feigned disinterest and let go. I wiped my hand on my trousers to remove what I hoped was hair gel. He looked the same as he had at school. He was shorter than me and had an unremarkable face. Still painfully thin and thrumming with nervous energy, he stood, his gaze jumping round the room from person to person before settling back onto mine. Anyone else would think he had taken a line of coke, but he was just like that. It seemed that apart from Will and me, he did not know anyone else, either.

"I'm surprised you haven't brought a book with you," he said drily.

The last six months of school had been weird for me, as I had struggled with the fact a huge part of my life was soon going to come to an end. It was also during this time that somebody had decided to torment me by tearing out the last page of any novel I brought to school. No matter where I had left my bag, the book I was reading, nestled safely between textbooks, would always have the final page missing by the time I got home. After this had happened to six books, I stopped bringing them to school. I could never prove it, but I knew it had been Rory. It was his style to be so vicious, to not let anybody have the satisfaction of knowing how a story turned out, happy or sad.

We stayed at the pub for a while before two taxis arrived to take us on to the next part of the stag do. We were going to engage in the manly art of warfare and splatter each other with pellets of paint. I managed to squeeze myself between a couple of Will's colleagues, who looked more suited for a game of rugby than paintballing. They all worked together in finance and exuded the brashness and confidence to match. A couple of them were already flushed from the booze. After half an hour, we were on the outskirts of Bristol by a warehouse in a rundown industrial estate. The other taxi pulled up next to us, and the group reunited with a round of backslapping. It was at this point that I almost pulled out. I could've gotten back in the taxi, turned around and gone to the train station. But I hesitated for too long trying to find an excuse and soon got ushered into the building with the others.

We were given overalls and face masks. I didn't know if I would be able to breathe properly. The testosterone rose as we were led into the cavernous warehouse, which had been converted into what I presumed was the aftermath of a bomb attack. Upturned cars and crumbling walls littered the floor, while ragged-looking two-storey structures took up space with interconnecting overhead gantries. It was a warren, but at least I could hide if I wanted to. I was determined to find somewhere as far from the action as possible.

We split into two gangs to play out three rounds. If a person was hit, it was over. The teams took opposite ends of the warehouse, and I went straight to the top of a structure, where I looked through a paneless window to watch the tableau unfold beneath me. The men whose normal battleground was the office were now assuming combat stances, barking orders at each other about offensive and defensive strategies, inadvertently giving away their locations.

"Fucking idiots," I muttered to myself as I watched the other team move forward in a pattern that was soon to encircle my team below. The first round lasted twenty minutes. The way my team handled themselves meant they were lambs to the slaughter, but I managed to pick off two men from my elevated position and emerged unmarked when the klaxon sounded. Before the start of the next round, our team huddled together and planned a strategy. I pointed out that more stealth was needed and could see a couple of men considering this novel concept. Our paint pellets were then changed to a different colour to set them apart from the splashes of the previous round. Simon suggested two men repeat my elevated position and assigned a ground troop to protect and cover, while he moved forward and drew the enemy to us. Thirty minutes later our team was celebrating. With the score equal, the mood turned serious as we knew the third and final round would be the decider. New alliances had formed and revised strategies were whispered from ear to ear.

Our team took positions at the far end of the warehouse. I pointed out that the enemy were now wise to our sniper positions, so we all agreed that getting behind and surprising them from this new position was the best option. The klaxon sounded, and we started creeping along the side walls of the warehouse, trying to be as silent as we could, inching our way round. With our watertight plan, we launched our assault as the enemy bottlenecked in a narrow area between two buildings. Our team hit five of their six men, but four of our team also went down in the crossfire. This meant if the remaining member of the other team managed to hit either Simon or me, then the entire game would result in a dead heat.

We fanned out, looking for their last remaining man. There were only a few minutes left. A flash of movement from an upstairs recess caught my eye, and I circled round to the stairwell beneath. I heard a sound above and crept up the metal steps. Before I reached the top, I could see the room. A figure was crouched, his back towards me, lining up the gun towards a target out on the warehouse floor. The figure tapped his right foot. I raised my pellet gun and gleefully emptied it onto Rory's back. The klaxon sounded. Our team had won.

An hour later, we were on a boat that was kitted out for a good time with a bar, speakers and plenty of tables. As we travelled back to the city centre, the men recounted their bravery in the field of combat, their voices becoming more raucous as they knocked back more beer. I would have enjoyed being on the river if it weren't for the bawdy laughter and terrible music on the boat. The scenery along the river was wasted on this lot. We eventually arrived at the quayside in the centre of Bristol, where Simon had organised a pub crawl.

We'd not long been in the first bar when a hen party came crashing through the doors. My heart sank. The women shrieked at a volume that eclipsed any noise we were making. Wrapped in boas and squeezed into tight dresses, the gaggle made a beeline for our group.

"It looks like the strippers have arrived," shouted one of Will's colleagues. I was mortified. The men roared with approval as the girls pretended to be offended, sweeping back their hair and preening their feathers. I moved farther down the bar as the women ordered cocktails, the names of which were full of sexual innuendos and contained liquid colours that matched their fake tans and make-up. I couldn't help but be judgemental, though they were probably all decent people. Maybe it was their confidence that put my nose out of joint, the way the men took charge and asserted themselves, elbows pointing outward, the jut of the male jaw, fanning out like a peacock displaying its feathers, loud voices and arrogant stances. The women were just as imposing. They could separate a male from the pack then pounce. One of the women had wrapped her boa around one of the stags, her hands on his thighs, while he sat on his bar stool pretending to ignore her.

I slipped outside for air and thought about going to find a phone box, so I could speak with Daniel, but the men emerged from the bar without the hen party in tow. We were on our way to the next bar already.

As we rounded the corner, a gay pub called the Shilling hove into view. The pavement outside was packed. As we passed, someone from our group hissed the word "faggot". Heads turned to look at us as one of the pub's customers quipped a camp retort. Will's colleagues laughed.

I felt like a traitor, especially as I thought overly affected campness damaged the reputation of living life as an average gay man. I did not want to be associated with "mincing queens" and effete behaviour used for shock value, because it embarrassed me. Owen was guilty of this, always loudly commenting on people in a disparaging fashion, deliberately intending to wound. Negativity, public shaming and confrontations...I hated it all. How hard was it for people just to be fucking *nice*?

I hung back to distance myself from the ugly flushed faces of the straight tribe I was now a part of. Their mouths twisted as they catcalled and jeered. When they were unable to match the wounding jibes thrown their way, I feared there might be violence. That scared me so I went to Will and told him to move on and drag his friends with him. He was appalled and paralysed as his friends goaded the gay men, who were now treating the verbal barrage as some sort of competition.

Simon appeared next to Will and me, equally shocked, until he went in to pull the colleagues out one at a time. The last person Simon dragged away was Rory. He grabbed his collar and pulled it back violently as Rory spat in the direction of a young man. I was utterly repulsed.

The stag party moved away and carried on, but I stayed where I was, watching them punch the air as they celebrated their apparent victory. Manhood checked and in place, they continued down the street, Rory bringing up the rear.

Will turned back and walked towards me. "Chris, I'm so sorry..."

"I'm heading off now."

He nodded. "I guess I'll see you at the wedding?"

I gave him a hug and turned back to walk to the station, the early evening still light. At the front of my mind was my plus-one guest. I wondered why I would place someone so precious in such vicious company.

Chapter Eleven

Daniel was clinging onto me tightly, his arms and legs wrapped around me. His bare body radiated an intense heat that made me sweat. I was on my back and he was on his side, his arm thrown across my chest, his fingers rising and falling as I breathed. I could feel the warmth from between his legs as he pressed against my hip and, farther down, our limbs were entangled. I couldn't be sure which were mine and which were his. His hair, golden even in the gloom, lay pooled around his head on the pillow. He drifted from sleep to wakefulness, his eyes half opened and focused on mine. A sleepy smile broke across his face, as bright as sunrise. It had been a week since we had first slept together, but we hadn't really spoken about it.

"I haven't told you my news," he said. "I spoke to my aunt yesterday when you were on the stag do. She's found something I might be interested in…"

My heart sank as I braced myself for the news he was moving out, but he told me something else instead.

"She found my father's contact details when she was packing. He's in the US."

"What? This is huge. What are you going to do?"

"I don't know. I might write him a letter... I haven't seen him since I was fourteen."

Daniel threw back the duvet and slid out of bed. I wanted him to climb back in with me, but I knew he had to get ready for work. I admired his naked body as he crossed the room and picked up a towel from a pile folded on a chair. He looked back at me and grinned as he opened the bedroom door. I was sure he was pleased that I was taking in every inch of him.

Now that he was out of sight, I heard him open and close the bathroom door, then the sound of the shower being turned on. I reached down under the duvet. I was semi-erect. The proximity of Daniel's naked body always did that to me. I idly played with myself as I recalled the night he had knocked on the door of this room, and I had invited him into my bed.

As Daniel sneaked beneath my sheets, a slight tremble ran through his body. I was nervous, too. I hadn't planned this, and there was no going back. What struck me immediately was the reticence on both our parts. With Henry, it had all been about drunkenly acting upon our basest carnal emotions and achieving quick sexual gratification. With Daniel, it was very different. We both lay there facing each other, letting the passing moments dictate our actions. I had stroked the side of his face and gazed into his eyes, in which moonlight from the window pooled. Daniel had reached over to run his hand down my back and over my behind, and pulled me closer to him. Our lips grazed against each other, and his eyes closed. We'd kissed reverently for what seemed an age, as our tongues became one in each other's mouths. It was slow and sensual, something to be savoured and lingered over. We'd both known we had all night.

Somehow the duvet was pushed off the bed. I had slowly pulled down his underwear, and now illuminated by the light from the clear night sky, the bed became a stage, and there we'd both lain, naked, with nothing to hide.

We'd never spoken a word. Maybe we had been scared that would break the spell? Time blurred and became an inconsequential thing. Days could have passed as I explored his body, caressing his thickening cock and the long ropey vein that ran down the length of it. We'd made love twice during the time it took night to blur into day. I was sure we had dozed at some point throughout but had awakened to more kisses until exhaustion had overtaken us.

* * * *

Ben and I were stacking books on the second floor when I told him about Oliver's drunken visit and how things had progressed with Daniel.

"I'm not sure what happens next. I don't know if it's a casual thing or not." I sighed.

"What's casual?" asked Tabitha, coming up the stairs.

"Chris has a boyfriend," Ben said with glee.

"What? No," I protested, as Tabitha squealed, patting my shoulders with excitement.

"Bring him to the book group," she said.

"Oh God…"

The book group was held every two months in the shop and involved copious amounts of after-hours wine.

"It would be perfect," she said, clapping her hands together. "We can all meet him, then we'll decide if he's the one for you."

"That sounds horrific, Tabitha. Anyway, he might be working."

The thought of them meeting Daniel made me nervous, as Tabitha had a knack for extracting people's life stories out of them within seconds.

When I got home, Daniel was reading on the sofa. I walked over and leaned over to give him a kiss. He tilted his head up to meet mine, and our lips met briefly. On the coffee table in front of him was a pile of scrunched-up writing paper and a fountain pen.

"I thought I would start writing that letter to Dad, but I don't know where to start."

I wanted to help, but I was out of my depth. I left Daniel to it, unsure of what he should do. Later that evening, I asked him to the book group, and he graciously accepted. He didn't seem at all flustered by the prospect, and I felt relieved.

* * * *

On Saturday we closed the shop half an hour early to set up for the event. As I draped a cloth over a low table, I felt a tap on my shoulder. When I turned, Oliver was standing in front of me wearing a look of contrition. He held his hands up in surrender.

"Before you say anything," he uttered, "I need to apologise. I shouldn't have thrown that bottle."

"It was awful. I don't know who that person was."

"To be honest, I scared myself. I am so sorry."

"Look. I should have told you Daniel was sleeping on my sofa, but I thought you'd take it the wrong way..."

"It was when he posted the ring back. That really got to me..."

I felt for him. "Daniel didn't know what to make of it," I explained. "You gave him an expensive gift after having only met him twice."

"I know. Will you apologise to him for me? Also, I want to give you this."

He placed an envelope on the table and walked away before I had a chance to reply. Inside was a cheque with a note explaining he wanted to cover the cost of the things he had broken. It was far too much — it would have paid for the broken picture frames ten times over at least.

Art was standing in the centre of the floor shouting instructions, while Tabitha brought down more chairs. Ben was running the vacuum cleaner around. There wasn't time to think about Oliver right now.

Just before six, Daniel turned up. "Will you be okay on your own for a bit?" I said to him.

"I'll be fine. I just met Art, by the way."

"Great." I hoped Art approved.

Although I enjoyed these evenings, it would have been nicer if Daniel and I had been here attending the event as guests. I left him to browse the shelves while I fussed around the people who arrived. The volume from multiple conversations increased, and as people settled into their seats, I scanned the room in search of Daniel. I spotted him talking to Tabitha and got worried.

As I approached, Tabitha was laughing. I rested my hand on his shoulder. "Oh God, what's she saying?" I asked, not joking.

"I was just asking Daniel a question that he wasn't sure how to answer," she said.

"What was that then?"

"Oh, I was just asking him if he thought you might want him as your boyfriend?"

I was mortified by her immature behaviour, like it was a game to her, to cover up for the cracks in her own dysfunctional relationship. This was the stuff of playgrounds.

"Well, that would depend on whether he would consider me boyfriend material," said Daniel quickly, sensing my shame. "I can cook. That should be enough."

They both looked at me expectantly. Maybe Tabitha's tactics were what was needed, after all. But there was no chance to reply because Art was now addressing the guests, shouting from the top of the staircase, his high-pitched voice piercing into the chatter in the room.

"I'd better sit down," said Daniel. He slipped off while Art introduced the evening's guest, the novelist Anna Hollister. Tabitha and I went to stand at the back of the room.

"Well, that was embarrassing. Did you plan that?" I hissed.

"No, but it wasn't a disaster, was it?" she replied. I couldn't argue.

We listened attentively as Anna spoke. I had loved reading her work ever since Art had recommended her to me several years ago. She was a bit of a local celebrity and also good friends with Art. After an hour and a half, Anna concluded her talk to rapturous applause. She had spoken for longer than we had anticipated and had only answered a few questions from the audience. She was now having a glass of wine with Art and talking to a small group of people who had closed in around her. There was a long queue of people at the till, all of whom had Anna's latest book in their hands, excited to get it signed. The evening had been a success.

At around ten, the guests started to leave. I went to find Daniel.

"What did you think?" I asked him.

"She was eloquent. I might try one of her books soon."

"Do you want to meet her?"

"Sure…"

He looked a little nervous as we approached Anna.

"Christopher! How lovely to see you." She kissed the air either side of my face, catching sight of Daniel.

"And who might you be?" she asked, taking his extended hand and shaking it, bemused at the formality of the gesture. He avoided a direct reply, and they indulged in small talk for a while. Tabitha and Ben had now left the shop. Only Daniel and I remained with Anna and Art.

"It's late, but we should all go for a bite to eat," Anna said. "A fun foursome, no?"

Five minutes later we were turning into a familiar cobbled street. I could sense Daniel's anticipation as Art held open the door to the restaurant. Inside, the waiter smiled, but said nothing as we were escorted to our table. Anna placed herself next to Daniel, who was now looking uncomfortable. The waiter came back to the table with a tray. "Kir royale on the house," he said, placing the drinks down. "Evening, Daniel," he added, setting a glass in front of him.

"Thanks, Harvey."

Anna placed her slim fingers on Daniel's arm and stroked it. "They like you in here."

Over the course of the meal, she paid far more attention to Daniel than she did to Art or me. She was attentive to all the details of his potted life history, but as he reached the part about working in Bath, I noticed he was embarrassed to talk about his job. He glossed over her questions and changed the subject. Just because she was an author, did he really think she was better than him? Maybe I wouldn't live up to his expectations, either. I could cushion myself from my own insecurities, but now I had to nurture someone else's. I picked at my food, half listening to Art recounting an anecdote, and tried to put myself in Daniel's shoes.

It was almost midnight by the time we finished our meal, and we were the only ones left in the restaurant. Anna was drunk, but we managed to slip away, leaving Art to make sure she got a taxi home. I felt bad for leaving him to it, but I couldn't get out of there quick enough.

Daniel was also drunk and started giggling as he linked his arm through mine. "Look what I've been given," he said, waving a piece of crumpled paper.

"She gave you her bloody phone number? When?"

"I told her I was gay, but that didn't seem to faze her. She said to call if I ever fancied a change. Don't worry. I've no intention of calling her. I told her I had a boyfriend."

He screwed up the number and lobbed it into a nearby bin before pulling me in closer. My head swirled with alcohol.

"We're really doing this, then?"

I wasn't sure if I had said it out loud or if it was just a thought. Casting my mind back to my first glimpse of him at Paddington Station, I was staggered by the enormity of where we were now.

Chapter Twelve

I knew it wouldn't be long before news about my new relationship got out at The Tap. I had to tell Oliver before he found out from somebody else. Daniel knew about the cheque, and we decided it wouldn't be right to take the money. I arranged to meet Oliver at lunchtime to tell him and give the cheque back, too. The way he thought everything could be put right by waving money around bothered me. However, I also felt somewhat to blame, as I hadn't been honest with him. Five hundred pounds was a lot, though.

I knocked on his door, the folded cheque digging in like a knife in my back pocket. Oliver let me in, and I went through into what he called his "drawing room". He set a glass of wine on the table and sat opposite me. The fact I hadn't been offered a drink spoke volumes. I remained standing and retrieved the cheque from my pocket.

"I want to give this back to you. It doesn't feel right."

I moved it across like a chess piece. He shrugged and took a sip of wine. "So how is our little friend? Is he still staying at yours?"

"Yes, he is. Things have changed between us. He's moved in." I'd decided that honesty was the best option on my walk up the hill, but I still wasn't sure how he would react.

"Well, that was fucking quick. These bloodsuckers don't wait around, do they?"

"Why are you so bitter?" I retorted. "You're the one that throws your money around, trying to buy people."

Oliver snorted. "That's rich coming from you. So I have lots of money. So what? Anyway, I don't buy people. I'm just generous. There *is* a difference. Unlike you, I don't play the emotional card every time I meet someone and tell them I'm a fucking orphan."

"Oh fuck you, Oliver." Hidden from view by the table, I curled my hands into fists, the nails digging painfully into my palms. There was jubilation in Oliver's eyes. He knew he'd hit a nerve.

"Poor, wounded Christopher. You lost your parents. Boohoo. Well, get over yourself. Everyone's parents die at some point. Mine are both gone too, you know? Big fucking deal! Who cares? Move on. It's getting boring hearing the same sob story. Grow up, Christopher, and get over it."

I wanted to kill him. It didn't help that he was clearly enjoying telling me some home truths.

"Their death doesn't make you some sort of saint," he continued, slouching back into his chair. "You're no saint. You pick up guys down at The Tap like everyone else does. Why are you so different from me? It's time you climbed down from your cross."

"So what if I pick up guys?" I countered. "That's not the issue here."

"Isn't it?"

"I treat them well. Unlike you, I don't throw people out onto the street at three a.m. or whatever, after having fucked them senseless on the living room floor," I said.

He smirked, then lit a cigarette. "At least I know what I want. You're scared of your own shadow and terrified of the prospect of any type of commitment whatsoever. You stay cocooned in your little flat, playing shops in that bloody bookshop with your weird friends. You never travel or go anywhere. There is a whole world out there. What's that about? Are you really so fucked up that you fear any emotional connection with another person? The difference between you and me, Christopher, is that I *choose* not to be emotionally engaged with other guys. I just want to have fun. What the hell is wrong with that? Just because you and your supposed morals disapprove of what I do, doesn't mean that I shouldn't do it. I've seen the way you look at me when I tell you about my little escapades. That roll of your eyes. The look of distaste, as if you've bitten into a rotten apple. That I can take. But the look of pity? That I can't. Who the hell do you think you are to make those judgements about me? You don't know me. You think you know me, but you don't. And, by the way, I'm hope you're proud of the way you fucking stole Daniel from me."

"You don't own him," I stated flatly.

"And neither do you," Oliver replied, without missing a beat.

The room fell silent. Oliver leant forward and took another sip of his wine.

"I'm sorry things didn't work out between you both," I said. "You're making it out that I pursued him after finding out he didn't want you, and that's not how it was. He was in a bad place, and I helped him out, then things changed."

Oliver looked pained. "Oh, here we go with the Mother Teresa sob story. Fuck off, Christopher. I don't want to hear about how you saved a lost soul. I might throw up."

"What do you want to hear, then?" I said indignantly. "I came here because I thought I owed it to you as a friend to give you an explanation about me and Daniel."

He sat back and gave me a cool assessing look. "Oh, we're not friends. You think you can absolve your sins by coming round here and giving me your version of events? See it from my point of view. I met Daniel and invited you to meet him, then it turns out that you two have met before. Then he decides he wants nothing to do with me. I hear nothing but silence from you until I turn up at yours and find him half naked in your flat. If you were in my position, what would you think? You poisoned him against me and then used your doe-eyed, woe-is-me story about your parents to reel him in for yourself. Are you really that pathetic and jealous of me that you have to steal my men just to make you feel better about yourself?"

"It wasn't like that!" I shouted. "He'd been fucking robbed and needed somewhere to stay. He stayed on my sofa."

"And then you started fucking."

I had no reply.

He reached over and picked up the cheque and tore it up. "Go home, Christopher. And when you're there with your little boyfriend, see if you can look him in the eye and convince him that you really are a good person. You can fuck off now. Please."

Most of my friends were acquaintances. I had never let them in. Art was probably the closest person to me, and that was because I was in no danger of falling in love with him. I was scared. I was scared of life. I was scared of commitment. I was scared of love. Oliver's words ran through me with each step that I took back towards Daniel. I knew I was broken. I missed my parents so much. Why wasn't that allowed?

Chapter Thirteen

Daniel was distracting me by seductively dropping morsels of salad into my mouth.

"Shall we just skip dinner and go to bed?" he offered.

"That would be nice, but I'm starving."

He leaned in and nibbled my earlobe, knowing it drove me crazy. I smiled despite myself. This was my favourite time of day, just home from work, knowing we had a cosy evening ahead of us. I couldn't remember the last time I had felt this happy. My entire world centred around him, and I wallowed in the fact that nothing else mattered.

The phone sounded, and I let it ring.

"Aren't you going to get that?"

I sighed and went to answer it, if only to halt the persistent din.

"Hello, is that Daniel?" said a voice I didn't recognise.

"No, hold on. I'll put him on."

Daniel was leaning against the cooker, picking at the salad.

"It's for you," I whispered to him, covering the mouthpiece. I closed the door and took my spot by the window in the other room. Daniel emerged forty-five minutes later.

"I didn't recognise my dad's voice," he said, his voice strangely toneless as he stood in the lounge doorway. "I could have been talking to a stranger. His accent had an American twang."

"Give it time."

"I know, but while Mum and I have been struggling, he's done all right for himself out there. He owns some company in LA, something to do with aerospace, I think he said."

I was sure that Daniel never realised that as he talked, his fingers danced erratically as they acted out his emotions. Right now, I could tell he was agitated. I gestured towards the sofa. He entered the room and perched stiffly on the edge of the cushion.

"I feel sorry for Mum. He was always out of the house early and late home. Even now I can picture myself eating at the table with her, my dad's chair empty."

"Did he say why he hadn't been in contact for so long?"

"Well, he was a bit defensive at first, saying since he had left, he had been busy building his company. He did remind me that he always sent me a birthday and Christmas card to Mum's address, though."

"Okay…" I was going to venture an opinion but told myself that it would be better if I just listened to what he had to say.

"He then asked me why I hadn't contacted him before, and why I had left it so long before sending a letter." Daniel wrapped his arms around himself and leant forward, his body rocking on the edge of the sofa. "Christopher, I could hear the hurt in his voice. It was awful."

He looked across the room at me sitting in the window seat alcove holding my knees to my chest. The anguish etched on Daniel face was heartbreaking. I swallowed the urge to remind him that it was his father who had abandoned his own family. After all, anyone can be quick to point the finger whilst being blissfully unaware of the missing part of the story.

Daniel sighed and stopped rocking. He made a concerted effort to relax himself and rested his hands upon his knees. The whites of his knuckles, though, were plainly visible. I waited till he was ready to continue.

"Anyway, as the years passed with no contact from me, he concluded I didn't want anything to do with him. As you can imagine, he was pretty angry when I said my mum never gave me his contact details." Daniel frowned. "I guess she had her reasons, though," he added, shrugging.

"Well, now you have the chance to make up for lost time, I guess. Get to know who your dad really is. Who knows?" I offered. "Maybe one day you could meet up with him?"

"That's how we ended the conversation. He wants me to go and visit him in Los Angeles."

"Oh wow...Fuck."

After all these years, he had this choice of whether or not to see his father again. I briefly imagined the same being true for me, and it felt like a jealous fantasy.

"I hope you didn't mind that he called me here. I put your phone number in the letter as an afterthought."

"Not at all," I replied, and gave him a reassuring smile. "I'm glad he called."

Daniel's mood had flattened since the phone call, and he was exhausted. I finished preparing the meal and we ate in silence at the dining table. He was distracted, and by nine-thirty he wanted to go to bed. I left him alone for a while, then went to the bookshelf, pulled out a book and took it with me to the bedroom. Daniel lay under the duvet, and since his back was to me, I couldn't tell if he was asleep. I switched on the lamp and angled it so there was just enough light for me to read by. I undressed quickly and went beneath the covers, propping myself up on my pillows. I reached out and stroked his back. He slid one of his feet across and rubbed it against the side of my right calf. I took the book, half the shimmering cover glowing in the light, the other half unintelligible, lost in the gloom. "*Songs of Innocence and of Experience* by William Blake," I read, turning to the first of the poems within. My voice was just above a whisper, enough to carry. I measured my pace and timbre, letting the words soothe him like a lullaby.

* * * *

A week later, we were walking through Victoria Park. He hadn't said much about the phone call, and I hadn't asked him.

"I'm angry at my mum for not telling me where he was. But my dad could have at least tried to write to me more often," he confessed.

"So what are you going to do?"

"I'm going to call him when I get back from work. They're eight hours behind us, so hopefully I'll catch him. I'll also try to call Mum again. See if she wants me to come home, but I doubt she will with Andy around."

Daniel and what was to come for him and his father had occupied my thoughts. I was worried his father might let him down even more or just keep him on the periphery. Daniel deserved more. And while I knew I couldn't get involved, I would still have to provide solace if he needed it. We also had to discuss what would happen when his aunt moved to Bristol, which was now a few short weeks away. Would he move in with her, or did he want to stay with me? I didn't want him to feel abandoned, but I didn't want to push him away by suffocating him with my affections. I felt like I was going mad.

Later that day, Daniel spoke to his father again and told him the visit would depend on the cost of the flight and getting the time off work.

"He said he didn't expect me to pay for my ticket, that he would sort that out," he said.

"Well, that's great. All you need to do is ask the restaurant if they can let you have some time off. How long do you think you'll go for?"

"Two weeks, maybe?"

"Hmm."

"You could always come, you know? Imagine the two of us in America. It would be an adventure."

I wasn't sure how to reply. Did I want to go on a father-and-son bonding trip? Having me there would complicate things.

"Shouldn't this just be all about you spending time with your dad? I would only be in the way. If you get on well this time, maybe I can come with you next time?"

"I knew you would say that."

This made me feel terrible.

"It's not about having quality time with a man I haven't seen for twelve years — it's a bit more than that. I need to know that if I reach out, you'll be there. I don't think you realise how much I need that in my life right now."

I was taken aback. "I'd love to go...but you should check if it's all right to bring someone."

"I already did. Dad has some time in early June, so I was hoping to go in a couple of weeks."

"A couple of weeks? That doesn't give me much time. Even if I could go, I'd need to get the time off work."

"I'm sure they can cope without you for a couple of weeks. You said yourself that Art is understanding... Plus, you need to go on holiday at some point in your life."

"Okay, let me check."

* * * *

The next day at work was quiet, as it had been for a while. It was clear it wouldn't be a struggle if I wasn't around for a couple of weeks. Art was running the ground floor. I flitted between the first and second floors. The sunlight flooded in through the front windows. Bright weather was not a friend to shop owners, as most people preferred to spend time in parks or gardens rather than browse indoors. During my lunch hour, I went for a wander through town. I stood in front of the travel agent's window looking at the cost of flights. Beautiful pictures accompanied the offers, tempting me with the promises I would receive if I travelled far and wide—crystal-clear lagoons, vast dunes and jungles, elephants, blue surf and cocktails. Daniel was right—I did need to go on holiday at some point in my life. Ten minutes later I had a list of dates and prices for flights from London to LA. I wanted to make the trip happen but still had to ask Art if I could get the time off. I was apprehensive about his answer, whatever it turned out to be, but if he said no, at least life would go on as normal.

Back at work, the shop was still devoid of customers, so I went to the travel section and took down a large atlas. I turned to the pages of America and the detailed maps of the east and west coasts. Certain place names stood out to me, because of songs or films—San Jose, and farther down, the wonderful-sounding San Luis Obispo. Tracing lower, I passed over Santa Barbara until I found Los Angeles and thought about how I could be walking through its streets for real in just two short weeks.

Art was in his office dealing with paperwork, which was spread in disarray across his desk. He had undone the top two buttons of his shirt, which usually meant he was stressed. Maybe now was not a good moment to ask for time off. His half-moon glasses were perched on his nose.

"Hello, Christopher."

"Art, I wondered…seeing as we're not busy, could I have two weeks off in June?"

"Why the urgency?"

I wasn't expecting that reaction, so I told him about Daniel's father and the offer to visit, then found myself revealing more, working backwards, explaining about the painful twelve-year gap in Daniel's life and the troubles his mother had endured after her husband left her. When I had finished, there was silence.

"Go book your flights."

"Will you be all right in the shop?"

"The three of us will manage just fine. Go book the flights."

* * * *

A ghost of a breeze passed through the evening air. With late spring almost over, there would be long summer evenings to look forward to. I walked along Brock Street and entered the grandeur of the Circus, the five majestic plane trees standing like silent sentries on the grassy inner circle. Around the outer circle, some houses had darkened windows, while others were bright with activity. I followed Daniel's route to work until I ended up on the cobblestone street. With time to kill until the end of his shift, I studied the dark windows of the shops, vaguely aware of some voices coming from the other end of the street.

"Christopher! Is that you?"

Two men approached.

"Henry?"

I walked up and hugged him. He looked more handsome than I recalled. His boyish smile and shaggy dark hair topped his muscular frame. As I scanned his body, my mind quickly flashed through the single night we'd spent together.

"This is David," he said, turning to his friend. We shook hands and chatted for a while, small talk. David then asked if I wanted to join them for a drink. Picking up on the intimation, I politely refused. Henry sensed my awkwardness.

"How about you go on in and get the first round?" he said to David. "I'll be over in a couple of minutes."

I waited until David was out of earshot. "You've got quite the obedient one there," I laughed. "Is he…"

"God no," Henry said. "We catch up now and then and have a few beers, and y'know… Where are you off to then?"

"I'm waiting for a friend."

He held his gaze over me for a second too long, and I bit my lip, not sure whether to mention Daniel by name. He moved in closer, and let his eyes roam lower down my body. I knew I could have had him.

"Lucky them," he said.

I stepped back.

"Another time then," Henry said. "I was hoping you might have called me."

"I know, I should have. A few things have happened…" I mumbled, not wanting to elaborate.

"So you met someone?"

"Yes," I admitted.

"I'm happy for you, although I would have liked to have seen you again." The hurt in Henry's voice did nothing to absolve any guilt I still had.

"We had a great night, didn't we?"

"We sure did. Look. If you still have my number, then call me…whenever. It was good to see you, Christopher."

"You too," I answered

We hugged, then he kissed me hard on the lips.

"Woah!"

He stepped back quickly. "I'm sorry. I shouldn't have done that!"

"I'll see you around, Henry. Go."

He walked away, leaving me reeling. I had bruised his ego, but I knew I wouldn't be able to stay in touch with him, even if it was only to maintain a friendship.

It was a few minutes past the hour. I arrived at the restaurant door just as Daniel sauntered out, his hands thrust deep into his jacket pockets. He stopped when he saw me.

"I wasn't expecting to see you here," he said, hugging me as tightly as Henry had just done.

"I wanted to surprise you. I have another surprise, too."

"So did you get the time off work?"

I smiled, and he kissed me.

"That's brilliant!" he said. "My dad thought it was a good idea to bring someone, actually. He has time off but will also have to work a little, too. He was worried I would be stuck home alone on those days."

"I take it you got the time off, too."

"Once I explained it was so I could visit my father and I hadn't seen him in twelve years, they couldn't really say no."

We approached the Circus, then headed towards the trees in the middle.

"I found us some flights, too," I said.

"Well, I guess it looks like we're going to LA, then." He grabbed my waist and lifted me up, pushing me back against a tree. The trunk was rough against my back. We kissed for a good while beneath the canopy of shadowed green, the soft rustle of the leaves applauding us for having come so far.

Chapter Fourteen

We were on a coach making our way to the airport at five fifty-seven in the morning, and it felt surprisingly good. I rested my hand on Daniel's leg as he took in the scenes that rushed by, the early June morning unusually overcast, the sky grey and featureless. He'd been quiet since we'd got on the coach, but I'd put it down to the fact he wasn't a morning person.

"You're miles away."

"I'm feeling a bit weird."

"Because of your dad?"

"I guess so, but I haven't ever flown before."

"What? But what about all that travelling you did?"

"We did it on a pittance," he said sheepishly. "We used trains and hitchhiked. Sometimes we just slept on the beach."

I was bemused by this revelation. Listening to him talking about his travels often left me feeling inadequate and jealous, but here he was, inexperienced and vulnerable.

"You'll be fine."

"I should have taken your advice and eaten something before we left."

I reached for an apple in my bag and gave it to him.

"Oh my God, it's like a fucking school trip." He laughed despite himself and leaned over to kiss me on the cheek, much to the disapproval of the old lady who was sitting in a nearby seat. He sank his teeth into the apple and juice ran down his chin. I swiped it with my finger and took in the momentary rush of sweetness.

The next couple of hours passed in a haze as we dozed, soothed by the steady rumble of wheels. At the airport, Daniel was like a kid fascinated by the rituals. As we checked in, he watched our suitcases disappear on the conveyor belt, marvelling that behind the scenes they had somehow made it onto the plane, but the seriousness of passing through security unsettled him, and he was nervous again.

Our plane was huge, which overwhelmed him. Daniel found the safety demonstration amusing, commenting about the silliness of a line of people spaced out at intervals, miming on a moving aircraft. As the plane skirted along the runway, I sensed his anxiety. His face was pale.

"There's nothing to worry about."

He didn't reply—his body tensed as the roar of the engines became louder, his hands gripping the arms of his seat. He screwed his eyes shut and reached for my hand as the plane lifted into the air. Eventually, the shaking cabin calmed as we were pressed back into our seats, the plane tilting upwards, rapidly gaining altitude. With difficulty, I managed to extricate my hand from his crushing grasp.

"I'm not doing that again," he said.

"Well, I'm afraid you're going to have to. You can't stay in LA."

The plane punched through the clouds and lit the cabin with sunlight. Daniel now seemed more relaxed, entranced by the view from the window, the world sliding past below. Seven hours later, we were flying over Canada.

He hadn't told his father we were together. I was a complete stranger to this man, yet here I was, about to stay in his house. Even though I didn't want to think about his reaction if and when he found out, it was still harder to live a lie compared to the consequences of the truth. I trusted Daniel to tell his dad when the time was right, but it didn't help my private anxiety. Now I was thinking that going on this trip had been a bad idea.

It was early afternoon when we started to descend. The sky was clear, and the sun was shining. Towns and suburbs passed beneath, giving way to pockets of desert. Huge interstates stretched for miles, like giant arteries carved into the earth. A constant stream of cars flowed along their surface, many turning off onto intermittent smaller roads that swooped in giant arcs, peeling off into another direction. The concentration of houses became denser, and from this height, a grid pattern was visible as we passed over blocks of residential areas. The plane banked sharply, changing our direction. In the distance was a small cluster of skyscrapers. The glass and steel shimmered in the heat.

The colour of the sky changed as we drew closer. The city's backdrop, a yellowish haze that hung overhead, reminded me of my sepia photographs back home. I'd heard about the air pollution here but had not realised just how visible it was. Seeing the packed freeways, I could now understand how the dirt got into the atmosphere. There was a clunk and rumble as we landed.

The first flight I had ever taken was with my parents when I was seven. We had been headed for Spain, and years later my father had told me how disappointed I had been when I had discovered the plane wasn't flying to outer space. I had bombarded him with questions that no parent had the answers to, and despite my mother's repeated attempts to hush me, I had carried on relentlessly over the course of the flight until all the nearby passengers were laughing. My father had told me good-naturedly that he had never felt so ignorant in his life.

"Are you ready?" I asked Daniel.

"If by ready, you mean nervous, then yes."

I let Daniel walk ahead of me as we passed through customs and emerged into a cavernous hall. We moved to the side so we wouldn't be in the way of the travellers behind us. Daniel scanned the crowds of people waiting to greet the arrivals.

"Do you expect he's changed much?"

"I'm sure I'll recognise him when I see him. He was blond like me, but that was twelve years ago."

I noticed a man threading his way through the crowd towards us. He was wearing a pale linen suit and a white shirt that contrasted against the glow of his tan. His iron-grey hair was cut short, and his white teeth were perfectly straight. I guessed that he smelled of citrus and cedarwood. He came right up to us.

"Hello, Daniel," he said kindly, before opening his arms.

* * * *

We were cruising in Alex's midnight-blue Mercedes. He had let the roof down as we emerged from the dimness of the airport car park into the Californian sun. At the airport, father and son had fallen into a tight embrace and Daniel had wept, which made me think about his father's pristine linen suit creasing. I was sad not to be able to comfort Daniel. All I could do was stand by and witness the reunion.

After father and son had broken apart from each other, Daniel introduced me to Alex. For a brief moment, I felt Alex assessing me in what I thought was a calculating way, until his disarming smile and warm handshake made me doubt what I had just seen. Daniel turned to me from the front seat, the thrill dancing in his eyes. I relaxed a little. It was impossible not to in this sun. I let my arm dangle over the side of the car and my fingers combed the wind as we followed signs north for the I-405 San Diego freeway.

Everything was so different. Wherever I looked, something grabbed my attention. The sensory overload was electrifying. The size of everything, the sheer amount of space used. We merged with the traffic on the freeway, and Alex closed the roof as I shrank back from the lumbering trucks, huge vans and cars that thundered along all seven lanes. On the opposite side of the freeway, another seven lanes of traffic drove towards us.

We continued driving, passing through different environments, wide streets lined with palm trees, fronds swaying in the breeze, towering high above us on elegant, tapered trunks. Alex pointed out the San Fernando Mountains that loomed in the distance, their green and brown barren contours contrasting with the colourful bustle and traffic down below. We wound through the network of streets, and at times were high enough to view LA laid out behind us like a vast shining carpet, the skyscrapers still visible farther back. We then drove past people's homes, with leafy trees lining the pavements, along with the ever-present palms. The houses were a mishmash of styles, yet all seemed to blend in with each other. The American flag was prevalent. The car slowed and turned into the driveway of a pretty one-storey house that sat back from the road, nestled in a copse of tall trees.

"Here we are, then," Alex said a little nervously.

Alex lived in Calabasas, in the northwest of LA in the San Fernando Valley. The neighbourhood was quiet, almost like it was expecting something. Pulses of spray danced from water sprinklers onto lush green lawns. The unmistakable aroma of fresh-cut grass perfumed the air.

We followed Alex into the house. The temperature was immediately cooler, and goosebumps started to prickle my arms. The entrance hall featured antique furniture and white walls with bright watercolours that detailed beach views. The kitchen was a vast hall of chrome and steel, the centrepiece a massive white marble-topped island.

"This is better than the kitchen at work," Daniel said.

Alex shrugged. "It was kitted out already when I bought the place. It's a bit much for one person. I don't need two ovens."

We continued down some stairs and into a vast oblong living area. The back wall was made of glass and looked out over a beautiful manicured garden where a navy-blue pool was waiting to be dipped into. Elevated decking with bamboo recliners overlooked the water. Tall trees framed the perimeter of the garden.

"This place is amazing," Daniel said.

In the centre of the room were two large sofas around an oval coffee table, its glass surface supported by a beautiful piece of driftwood. Striking blocks of abstract art added colour to the walls, while a modest TV hid in the corner. Tall plants stood proud in copper pots throughout the room. Drifting from object to object, I realised my entire flat was smaller than this room alone. Was Daniel also comparing his home in Bath to this one? It was easy to admire what we couldn't have, but did this actually belong to Daniel?

Towards the right of the room were even more steps leading up to a dining area that could easily fit twelve people. Alex folded back a pane of the glass wall until it was open to the garden.

"You'll be staying out here," he said, stepping out beneath a pergola.

"We're camping outside?" Daniel said.

Alex's eyes creased with amusement, the only folds apparent on his unlined face. He walked us over to another building past the pool.

"No, you'll be staying in the guest cottage. There are two en-suite bedrooms, a lounge and a small kitchen. Make yourselves at home."

"Okay."

"I don't expect you to stay here all the time. I hope we will spend most evenings in the main house."

I was relieved that we would be sleeping out of the main house. I looked at the double beds in each bedroom. I would find it hard knowing Daniel was on the other side of a wall.

"I'll let you unpack, then," Alex said. He moved towards Daniel and hugged him briefly, "It's good to have you here, son."

He disappeared and left us both standing in the cottage, a little stunned.

"Well, this is surreal," I said, walking from room to room.

"It's past midnight back home, but I'm not tired yet. I'm buzzing."

"Are we going to have to sleep in separate bedrooms?

"I'm sorry, but it just didn't feel right telling him over the phone."

"I know. I understand."

He walked over and kissed my ear, sending a tingle through my body. "Of course we can share a bed. Dad won't walk in."

"I hope not."

"I *will* tell him, but only when it feels right. After twelve years, it's just not the first conversation I want to have with him face to face."

"I know. It just feels a bit unnerving having a secret from someone, especially when you're staying in their house."

We went to Daniel's bedroom. He started hanging his clothes in the wardrobe, making himself at home.

"To be honest, although we haven't seen each other for so many years, I always remember Dad being very liberal, so I hope it won't be a problem. Don't forget, LA is pretty relaxed towards gay people. He would hardly live here if he disagreed."

I felt dirty and wrinkled after the flight, so I went to take a shower in my own bathroom, which was more of a wet room with no glass partitions, just a recessed drain in the floor. The walls and floor were tiled with large slabs of honey-coloured travertine stone, the surfaces flat and polished. I let the water revive me, relishing the shiver it sent through me. As I reached for my shower gel, I wondered if I should ask Daniel to join me, or was it too risky? Before I could decide, Daniel appeared in the doorway and stood there watching me. I beckoned him over. He quickly undressed, his trousers and underwear pooling around his ankles, and within moments he was with me under the spray, rubbing my chest and torso.

"Why don't you let me do that?" Daniel murmured, nuzzling his lips against my neck, and taking the bottle from my hands. He squirted out a generous globule of gel into one hand and started to lather up my chest.

After a minute, I took the bottle back from him. "Turn around," I instructed. Daniel obediently obeyed, and I soaped up his back, watching the hot spray wash the lather away. Daniel turned his face up into the jet of water, and a waterfall cascaded down the back of his head, his hair flattened against his neck. He arched his back as he stretched, and I admired the architecture of his frame.

I ran my fingers unhurriedly over the contours of his shoulder blades and down his spine, his long torso seemingly going on forever. Farther down, I stroked the twin mounds of his buttocks. Daniel flexed them playfully, the soft flesh turning to marble.

He turned around and pressed himself up against me. His erection was swelling and growing thicker.

He leant closer, and sucked on my earlobe, knowing all too well that it would make me shudder with delight. I moaned with pleasure and reached down to grip Daniel firmly between his legs. He gasped and leaned over to adjust the temperature controls.

"I think we need to turn the heat up in here," he breathed, gluing his mouth to mine. We kissed passionately and with urgency, our hands increasing in rhythm as we pleasured each other. It didn't take long for us to climax at the same time, and I gripped the back of Daniel's head, his muffled cry muted, as his lips remained fused to mine.

I turned off the water and rested my head against his shoulder, both of us panting. Across the room I could just make out our blurry reflection in the mirror above the sink, our images fading in the enveloping steam.

We patted ourselves dry with towels, and shakily moved back into the bedroom, where we lay naked on the bed to catch our breath, sated.

"We'd better go to the main house soon," Daniel said after a while.

"Do you want to go ahead?" I offered. "You should spend some time alone with your dad. I can stay here."

Daniel turned towards me and shook his head. "I'm really nervous. What do we talk about? It's like meeting a stranger for the first time" He reached down and took my hand. "I'd feel much better with you there. Maybe you could fill any gaps if the conversation becomes stilted?"

"I'll give it my best shot, but I can't promise anything. You'll be fine," I assured Daniel, with a squeeze of his hand. "Concentrate on those things you can remember about him. Don't forget, he's probably as nervous as you are." I gestured for Daniel to get up. "Come on. It would be rude to keep your dad waiting. Let's get dressed."

Closing the cottage door behind us, we went through into the bright garden. Alex was waiting for us under the pergola. I wondered how long he'd been there. Had he been outside the entire time Daniel and I were in the shower, or lying naked on the bed? Three wicker chairs formed a loose circle round a wrought-iron table, the top decorated with navy and cream tiles. Alex wore a white T-shirt that clung to the contours of his chest and exposed the muscles on his bronzed arms, the hair on them bleached gold by the sun. The heady scent of jasmine drifted towards us from above, where the small white flowers were dotted among the canopy.

Alex told us about his work, focusing the conversation towards his son, who asked keen questions. He touched briefly on Joanna but soon glossed over the topic. He asked me about my life and work, too, and I revealed just enough to be interesting, but not enough for him to think I wouldn't be good enough for his son.

"Is there anything you don't like to eat?" he asked.

"Nope. We'll eat anything and everything," Daniel replied.

"So you still have a big appetite then? You used to eat so much when you were a kid."

We went through to the kitchen and watched as Alex prepped some vegetables.

"I can't remember you cooking," said Daniel.

These words made me tense. Although innocent on the surface, the comment was loaded, too. I looked at Daniel sharply, but he didn't notice. He had told me that when his dad had been living at home, Alex had existed on reheated meals late at night after the rest of the family had gone to bed. Was Daniel impressed or annoyed that his father had now bettered himself by learning to cook, or was he wondering why he hadn't done it years ago and been at home more?

"Well, once I was out here, I had to learn how, pretty quickly."

He went to the hob and tipped some seafood into the wok, where it sizzled. "Since moving to LA, I've discovered a passion for cooking. Healthy food and a healthy lifestyle is very much the thing around here. Although there are still a few things I like to indulge in."

We watched as he added spices — the way he performed it was delicate, like a sorcerer crafting a potion, meticulous and diligent. Daniel helped cook the pasta and finish the salad, ready for Alex to portion everything out into bowls, which we carried outside.

Alex moved his hands in the air in the same way as Daniel's did when he spoke, except there was more confidence. He told us about how he had explored the city when he had first arrived here. "Tomorrow you should rest and use the pool. I'll show you around some places the day after," he said.

It was getting late, and the burden of the day was hitting me hard. I stood up to announce I was going to bed, even though I sensed Daniel wanted me to stay. My sleep came fast, but somewhere in the drift of my consciousness, I knew Daniel had joined me in bed, his arm protectively wrapped around my chest. As I stirred, the last thing I heard was the gentle rhythmic sound of the male cicadas, their mating call lulling me back to sleep.

Chapter Fifteen

For a moment, I did not know where I was. The room was semi-dark, with daylight smeared along the walls of the hallway just within view of the opened bedroom door. It still felt early, but I was alone in bed. The covers were thrown back on the side opposite me, the bottom sheet creased, marking where Daniel had slept. I went to the bathroom and urinated for what seemed like an eternity. Daniel's grey shorts hung on a rail, so I slipped them on and wandered outside towards the pool. The surface of the water repeated staccato choppy waves as Daniel's long limbs effortlessly glided back and forth. I admired the way the muscles in his shoulders and back flexed. He stopped at the pool's edge and heaved himself out. Rivulets of water slid down his body.

"Have you seen Alex this morning?" I asked as he dried himself off.

"Not yet. I heard a car engine a while ago. He might have left for work already."

His father leaving early and returning late was what he was used to.

"It was good of him to pick us up and cook for us yesterday. He's gone to a lot of trouble."

"I know. He's trying hard to make amends... Why don't you have a swim?"

I went back to the bedroom to change into my swimming trunks. When I went back to the pool, Daniel was talking with a woman under the pergola. She was attractive, with chestnut-coloured hair and a pale figure-hugging dress that skimmed just above her knees. She dangled a large pair of dark sunglasses from her left hand, although a cigarette would have worked just as well. She was laughing at something Daniel had said.

"Hello, I'm Christopher."

She smiled warmly. "I'm Juliette. It's a pleasure to meet you."

She had a European accent, not the American twang I was expecting. Her words were eloquently shaped and seemed even more sophisticated framed by the sheer plum-red lipstick that complemented her cascade of hair. Her gaze held mine in a friendly yet measured way. I felt very underdressed in just my trunks.

"I've just dropped by to pick up some paperwork for Alex, but I wanted to say hi."

She turned and walked back into the house, leaving us standing there.

"That was weird," said Daniel tersely. "I wonder if she's seeing my dad?"

"Maybe."

"It's not as if Dad shouldn't see anyone, but you would have thought he would have said something if he was."

"Well, maybe he's waiting for the right moment?"

* * * *

We spent the morning by the pool, staying shaded from the sun. We dozed, our bodies still trying to acclimatise to the time difference, but eventually hunger got the better of us and we went to the kitchen in the main house and helped ourselves to ingredients from the fridge.

"I've worked in quite a few kitchens, but I haven't a clue what half these gadgets are for," said Daniel, opening cupboards and drawers. "I've got an idea... Let's have a look around the house."

It felt like trespassing, but at the same time I was curious. We went into the sitting room, where the vaulted ceiling towered above us. The natural grain of the wooden arches stood out against the stark white of the walls, which in turn enhanced the vivid blocks of art. Modern art had never interested me, but these pictures were striking, and there were many oversized canvases filled with different hues of a single colour. On the far wall was a dark blue painting, rendered in oils, the undulating surface mimicking the sea. Midnight-blue rose from the bottom right and married other shades in an energetic swirl, until transforming into an inviting aquamarine. The initials "L.B." subtly graced the corner. The next piece was vivid in cadmium yellow, while the piece next to that displayed a torment of violets and black.

Daniel scanned the bookcases. "Look at all these books on art. Since when is Dad interested in all this stuff?"

There were also books on military history and aviation, but no fiction. We went into the dining room, all glass and darkened chrome. It was incredibly formal, which made me wonder if anyone had ever had a good time in there. It had the air of a boardroom, detached and clinical with no warmth or intimacy.

"So he could never find the time to eat with Mum and me, but now he hosts dinner parties?"

We headed back to the kitchen along a newly discovered corridor. Daniel tried various handles, which revealed even more bedrooms, silent and unused. We turned a different corner, and another door opened. The room contained a huge mahogany desk with a large computer on top. More bookcases lined the walls. I stepped over with the air of a trespasser. The books were mainly technical manuals. Behind the desk was a wall covered with framed certificates and photos of Alex being presented with awards. Daniel looked at each frame in turn, his eyebrows raised.

"Let's get out of here," he said.

There was one more door at the end of the corridor, Daniel pushed down on the handle and went in. I followed.

"Do you think we should be in here?" I asked, standing at the foot of Alex's bed.

"I just want a quick look, that's all."

The room was decorated in muted greys and featured industrial-style furniture. It was a smart minimalist space, yet clearly modelled on the aesthetic of his working environment. There was nothing that gave a clue as to who lived here, apart from someone who was married to their work and was comfortable in a masculine environment. The one splash of colour was a painting of a female nude that hung above a chest of drawers. The background was a deep vivid red. The woman had been captured dancing, her arms above her head, her eyes closed. I felt like an interloper, intruding on her private reverie. Daniel called out to me from the en-suite bathroom, and I went over. He pointed at the two toothbrushes by the sink with a shrug.

* * * *

Alex returned home at seven. "Sorry I didn't see you this morning. I had to get to the office early," he said. Daniel stayed silent. It had been twelve years. He was no longer a boy, and Alex was living an affluent lifestyle. They each had to learn who the other was, all over again.

"Tell me about your day," Alex said, placing three beer bottles on the table under the pergola.

Daniel left me to prop up the conversation. I told him the brief version, omitting the visit from Juliette and snooping around the house.

"The garden is so beautifully secluded. It's as if we're shut off from the rest of the world," I said.

"That's one of the reasons I bought it."

"We had a visitor," said Daniel, leaving the statement hanging in the air.

"Was it the gardener?" asked Alex, frowning. "I told him not to come today."

"No, it was someone else…Juliette." Daniel drew out each syllable as he spoke her name. "She looked like she had just walked off a movie set."

"Oh, you met Juliette? She was just grabbing something from the office in the house. She works for me." Alex relaxed back into his seat and reached for his beer.

"Does she?" countered Daniel, his tone clipped and abrasive.

"Yes."

"Is that who you left us for?" Daniel stared at his father, daring him to answer.

"No, Daniel," Alex said patiently. "I never left your mother for anyone else."

"Really? Why should I believe you? You were never around. You could have been anywhere," argued Daniel.

"We were just naturally drifting apart. I know that I'm at fault and that my job was all-consuming. It still is." Alex raised the bottle to his lips and drank.

"You don't need to remind me about that. But did it ever cross your mind that we might have needed you?"

"Your mother didn't want to move when I got offered the job in LA. She offered me an ultimatum — the marriage or my job," replied Alex, his voice calm and measured.

"You put her in that position."

"I could have provided a better life for us all out here. She just couldn't see that."

"Better life for us all?" mocked Daniel. "We wouldn't have seen you but just been stuck out here with no friends or family. Even worse than home."

"It was an agonising choice, Daniel. But to be honest, I don't think she thought I had the balls to go through with it. Maybe she was bluffing." Alex placed the beer bottle back on the table and wiped his hand on his trousers.

"You have no idea what it did to her when you left. She started drinking every single fucking day. I had to spend *two years* after uni helping her out of depression. I worked extra jobs just to pay for her counselling while you were lounging by this fucking pool," said Daniel angrily.

Alex looked taken aback. "If I had known what was happening, I would have helped. It was *her* decision to make sure I was removed from your life."

"And why do you think she did that? Probably to protect me from the fact your work was more important than your family," Daniel retorted.

"The only communication I ever had was your new address after you moved out of our old home. She wrote a short note saying to send you birthday cards and Christmas cards, but that was it. I didn't realise you didn't know about that."

"I don't believe you," Daniel replied petulantly.

"I paid child support up until your eighteenth birthday, and, after that, all I could do was hope that you would want to get in contact. Don't paint me out to be the bad guy here, Danny," said Alex, a warning note creeping into his tone.

Daniel leant forward, his elbows resting on his knees, his hair hanging down, obscuring his face. "I was so angry with you. When Mum became a mess, I was the one who had to pick up the pieces."

"I was always there for you. Please understand," pleaded Alex.

"Why are there two toothbrushes in your bathroom?"

"You've been in my bedroom?" Alex raised his eyebrows in surprise.

Daniel slouched back in his seat, sullen yet strangely jubilant. He had caught his father out. "What aren't you telling me, Dad?"

I rose from the table, but Daniel motioned for me to sit. Alex sat there, stony faced. "You get to start a great new life without looking back. Meanwhile, I rescue Mum from alcoholism and depression, and then she goes off with a man who likes to beat her black and blue."

"What?"

"Yes. He put her in hospital and threw me out of my own fucking home. I was homeless — homeless while you're living in this fucking palace," spat Daniel.

As Daniel gestured wildly, his hand sent a beer bottle flying across the flagstones, shattering brown glass towards the edge of the pool, but he didn't even notice. His eyes filled, and without another word, he stood up and walked towards the cottage.

I moved my chair back. "I should go and see him."

"Stay here. Give him some time. He used to do this when he was a kid...have these rages. He needs to be alone," said Alex, his voice devoid of emotion, as his gaze followed Daniel's retreating back.

Chapter Sixteen

The storm had dissipated as quickly as it had arrived, and the following day, Alex and Daniel were back on speaking terms. If I had been on the receiving end of Daniel's outburst like Alex had, I would have been hurt. It reminded me of the last time I had seen Oliver.

Part of me was conflicted — it was embarrassing seeing Daniel act like a child — but realising how well his father knew him, despite not being part of his life for twelve years, made me feel even more like I shouldn't be here. Daniel was so new to me. That evening Alex offered to take us out for dinner at his favourite Mexican place.

"It was my fault," Daniel admitted, as we got dressed ready to go out. "I was too harsh, trying to find out if that Juliette woman was who she claimed to be."

"It's understandable."

"I think both my parents are to blame, really. I was just caught in the middle. I can't take sides any more. I need to come out of this having salvaged something."

An hour later, the three of us were cruising through Calabasas. The evening sun had turned everything it touched to gold. The assortment of different architectures and styles was intriguing. White grand curving houses, their façades all pillars and arches, abutted modern minimalist cubes, the sharp corners of darkened glass and steel reflected in their infinity pools. Farther on were Spanish haciendas with manicured gardens that glowed under hidden spotlights.

I was hoping that the meal would be a much calmer affair than the previous evening's showdown. Alex had booked a table at the small restaurant. The décor was austere, the uneven whitewashed walls strung with tiny bulbs casting a warm glow across the room. A whisper of music underscored the murmur of conversations from surrounding tables. I had tried Mexican cuisine before, but looking at the food being carried from the kitchen to nearby tables, I knew we were in for a treat this evening. It struck me how clever Alex had been by taking us out for dinner. Here we were on neutral territory, and as we settled into our surroundings, both Daniel and Alex started to relax.

"This menu has too many choices. I want it all," Daniel complained.

"Can you remember that restaurant that your mother and I used to take you to whenever we had a family celebration?" Alex asked, looking over the top of his menu at Daniel, who was sipping from his water glass.

I was bemused as Daniel spat out a small mouthful of water. He started coughing then dissolved into laughter, closely followed by Alex.

"The waiter…" Daniel couldn't continue as he collapsed into giggles.

Alex's shoulders were hitching up and down, and he clasped a hand to his mouth. He must have noticed my befuddled expression.

"Sorry, Christopher. Poor Daniel and I used to get in so much trouble whenever we went there."

Daniel turned to me. "We used to go to this restaurant for birthdays or whatever, and they always had the same waiter working there. I don't think he ever had a day off. Anyway, he had grey hair at the sides of his head, but for some reason, he wore a toupee that was jet black, and it perched on top of his head like a bird's nest. Every time we went in, Dad and I wouldn't be able to stop laughing at how ridiculous it looked, and Mum would get really angry with us both."

"Oh, and the food!" said Alex, sounding pained. "They used to offer a glass of tomato or orange juice as a starter or half a grapefruit that would slide round your plate."

I wasn't expecting that they would talk much about when they were a family of three, but hearing them reminisce with such humour made me hope that last night's altercation was a one-off incident…a venting of bubbling emotions that'd been simmering beneath the surface for a long time and now had been released. Maybe this sharing of past times would bring them closer once more.

Alex ordered us margaritas, which he promised were the best in California. He stuck with a bottle of beer with the obligatory wedge of lime in the top.

The table grew silent once our food arrived. We shared our order of quesadillas and enchiladas and helped ourselves to refried beans and guacamole.

"Dad, this food is amazing. How did you find this place?" exclaimed Alex, scooping up fresh salsa with a tortilla chip.

Alex took a swig of beer before answering. "I've been coming here for years. It was one of the first good restaurants I found. When I arrived in LA, I ate out a lot until I learnt the basics of cooking. I used to drive around each night after work. It's a big city, and I needed to get my bearings, so I'd explore different areas and find new places to eat." He pushed some food around his plate with his fork. "It used to beat rattling around an empty apartment, feeling lonely and sorry for myself." Alex looked up quickly. "Not that I'm looking for any sympathy. I'm a firm believer in that if you make your bed, you have to lie in it."

Daniel nodded and sat back in his chair, his gaze fixed on his father.

"To be honest, Dad, although I've travelled abroad a bit, I'm sure I'd find it pretty terrifying living alone in a different country." He paused. I could see he was thinking about what to say next. Daniel glanced at me before continuing. "Although I can't condone you leaving us the way you did, I have to say that I admire what you've achieved all by yourself."

Alex put down his cutlery and blotted his mouth with his napkin. I sat stock still, hoping this was not going to be the beginning of another row.

"Danny, I understand completely what you are saying, but one day I hope you will understand why I left. Let's not ruin a nice evening arguing over who is right or wrong." Alex let out a long sigh before continuing. "I appreciate your words about my achievements, but most of those are bittersweet. Once I arrived here, I missed you so much that all I could do to alleviate the pain was to bury myself in my work, night and day."

I felt like an interloper sitting there. These words were not meant for my ears, so I quietly focused on the food on my plate. Daniel stayed silent.

"In recent years, I'd all but given up that I would ever hear from you again. I had to sit down after I opened up your letter." Alex let out a little laugh. "Even now, I can't believe you're here. Thank you for coming."

I looked up to see Alex hold out his beer bottle. Daniel picked up his drink and clinked it against his father's. They smiled shyly at one another.

The rest of the meal was spent in happy recollection. Alex and Daniel gently teased each other as they drew from memories of a different life that they had once led together. They did their best to include me, but I was happy to sit back and watch father and son taking those tentative steps to bond again.

* * * *

As we left the restaurant, the night air had cooled to offer a pleasant respite from the heat of the day as we made our way home and to bed.

At three a.m., I absently reached down to stroke Ptolemy, but he was not there. I hoped he was behaving for Margaret, my neighbour back in Bath, who I had trusted to take care of him. I slipped out of bed, grabbed a book then headed to the lounge to curl up on the sofa. I read for a while but must have fallen asleep. When I roused, the light outside was brighter than before. It was now approaching six a.m.

The flagstone path was damp and, as I stepped onto the grass, my feet became wet, as the sprinklers had just finished their morning ritual. The air was fresh and full of birdsong. I moved closer to the pool and sat by the edge. An anticipatory shiver ran through me as I lowered my legs into the water. I was expecting it to be cold, but it was warm compared to the morning air. I removed my shorts and lowered myself into the water, relishing the feel of the water against my naked body. The thrill of doing something so risqué was exhilarating. I swam a few experimental laps, moving slowly through the water so as to not make any noise. After a few minutes, I was out of the pool and back into my shorts. The air was not yet warm enough to dry me.

Daniel was still asleep. The sheets had been kicked down lower, exposing his back and the beginning of the gentle rise towards his buttocks. I sat on the edge of the bed and leant forward. A splatter of water droplets fell from my hair and dotted his back. He moved lazily, emerging from sleep with a groan, and reached around trying to discover what had woken him. I bent down and kissed his shoulder before moving lower and licking one of the drops of water off his back.

"Mmm, that feels nice." His voice was muffled by the pillow, like he had a mouth full of cotton wool. He turned over and stretched, his eyes slowly opening. More water pattered onto his chest and stomach.

"Hey, you're all wet," he said sleepily.

"I know. I just went skinny dipping," I replied.

Daniel arched a disapproving eyebrow at me. "Don't let my dad catch you doing that."

* * * *

Later that morning, we left Calabasas for Mulholland Drive, the radio providing a soundtrack as Alex drove. The route took us across northern LA and climbed and dropped, snaking and winding around the contours of the hills. Occasionally we took a bend and passed huge imposing mansions nestled back from the road, protected by high gates and perimeter fences. We passed Coldwater Canyon. I drank in the scenery as each new view presented itself as perfect as a picture on a postcard. It reminded me of the hills that surrounded Bath back home. I had spent many late summer evenings upon hilltops gazing down at the city lights below. We moved towards the Hollywood Hills, stopping to take in the grand vista of Studio City and Universal Studios that lay far below.

"I remember driving up and looking at this view after I moved here," said Alex. "I used to wonder what you were doing, and I hoped you were okay. Not a week went by when I didn't think about you and miss you." Daniel smiled, and I felt relieved.

We were soon cruising a wide highway, neat with well-watered grass verges and elegant palm trees. It was very alien, and for a moment, I craved the familiarity of Bath with the sights and sounds of my usual life. I couldn't imagine living here. Daniel, on the other hand, now seemed at ease. As we passed the Hollywood Bowl, he pointed to his left. In the distance, miles away, were the letters that formed one of the most iconic signs in the world. I hastily took a few shots with my camera, hoping for the best.

We arrived at the Griffith Observatory, an imposing white building with heavily patinated old copper domes. We climbed some stairs that took us level with the base of the domes, then passed through a number of arches until in front of us lay an unforgettable view. The dense greenery of scrub and trees undulated down and fanned out into the sprawl of the city below. The sheer size of it shimmering away in the heat down below was staggering. The city spread out in every direction before blending into the haze of distant mountain ranges. I reached for my camera. Daniel was standing very close to his father, hemmed in by the surrounding tourists, and I included them in my picture as they looked out at the scene. I wanted Daniel to see it from my point of view.

Alex threw his arm around his son's shoulders as he started pointing at places of interest in the distance. "See those skyscrapers over there? That's the financial district. Down here to the right is Sunset Boulevard, and behind it are Paramount Studios."

Daniel followed his dad's outstretched arm as it panned from left to right, and I felt a twinge of sympathy for Alex, who was trying so hard to reconnect with his son again.

Having now seen a different side of Daniel, I suspected that it would be a long time coming before he would forgive his father for leaving him. I just hoped there would be no further scenes like before.

"I bet it looks even more impressive at night," said Daniel, raising a hand to shield his eyes from the overhead sun.

Alex nodded. "I attended a fundraiser up here one evening years ago, one of those black-tie events. I remember coming out onto this exact spot and looking down with awe at the city at night for the first time, all lit up like a Christmas tree. It always reminds me of a giant runway that recedes into the distance, waiting for planes to land."

Daniel turned to his dad. "I'd love to see that."

"It's pretty special. I'll bring you up again sometime. C'mon. Let's go. There's plenty more that I want you to see."

We left the observatory and drove along Hollywood Boulevard, passing the tourists as they posed for photos outside the Walk of Fame. I was impressed with Alex's knowledge of LA. He rattled off place names and pointed out landmarks, all the while navigating the busy streets, unfazed by the busy traffic. We followed Santa Monica Boulevard through Beverly Hills and down to the pier. The sun was constant, casting the odd dappled shadow, flitting through the huge palm fronds that flanked us on both sides of the street.

At Venice Beach, the boardwalk was filled with crowds. Skaters wove effortlessly among us, some dressed flamboyantly as if wearing a stage costume, while others were dressed for the gym. Tourists mingled with locals, their presence welcomed here. A group of sun-kissed teenagers passed close by, surfboards under arms. I could see the crystals on their skin where the saltwater had dried in the balmy air.

We passed a large concrete skateboard park. The skaters skittered around like ants, all trying to outdo each other, long hair flying as they hoped for the impossible on their boards. Pumped-up bodybuilders exercised and flexed, all preening like peacocks, sweat running down their faces, their muscles resembling huge burnished slabs of brown marble, glistening in the sunlight. As we passed, Alex looked at them, self-consciously touching his own arms. Like the promised wonders of a circus poster, I was excited and not sure what to expect next. It was a very long way from home.

Alex pointed out a building up ahead. It was a small restaurant with a bar area that spilled out into the street. It had a tropical vibe, and all the tables and chairs looked like they had recently been washed ashore, with blistered blue paint covering some of the weathered surfaces.

"Let's grab a drink," he said, signalling to a waiter. Once seated, Alex ordered some beers and a few small plates of fresh seafood.

"So is this how you spend your weekends, Dad?" Daniel asked, his gaze focused on the steady stream of people ambling up and down the boardwalk in front of us.

"God, no. I'm usually too tired. I try and come to the coast at least once a month, but I do tend to find myself in the office for a few hours on a Saturday or Sunday. I seem to get a lot more done with no one else around."

Alex scratched the stubble on his chin. I thought it suited him.

"So you still work as much as you did when I was a little boy?"

Alex didn't answer straight away. He cocked his head slightly and fixed Daniel with an impenetrable look. I wondered if he thought, like me, that this was a loaded question that would lead to another barrage of accusations and a war of words. Daniel was oblivious, still people-watching.

"I try not to work as many hours as I did when I first moved here," Alex said. It sounded like he was choosing his words carefully. "I suppose old habits die hard, but I do now make a concerted effort to take time out to appreciate who and what are important to me in my life. That's why it's so great that you're here."

Our drinks and food arrived before Daniel could answer. We helped ourselves to shelled shrimp and cracked lobster claws, mopping the sauce up with crusty white bread.

"How about you two? Do you get weekends off together?"

I immediately tensed. The way he phrased it sounded to me like he assumed we were a couple. I glanced at Daniel. It could have been my imagination, but for a moment he too seemed on edge.

"We don't really see that much of each other," I said, trying to sound nonchalant. "Daniel tends to work most evenings, and I usually work all day Saturday or Sunday. It's one of the joys of working in the retail and service industry."

Alex laughed and nodded. "Along with wearing a smile on your face all day, I presume? I take my hat off to you both."

"I actually enjoy it, Dad," said Daniel, leaning forward. "I've learnt a lot about food and wine. The tips are good, too. I'm happy there for now. As for Christopher, you should see how many books he's got. Most days he comes back having bought new ones. He's very well read."

I could feel myself starting to flush and swigged the last of my beer from the bottle.

"I'm glad you both enjoy your jobs," said Alex. "Just remember it's important not to stagnate. It'll be interesting to see where you'll both be working a few years from now."

I raised my eyebrows at Daniel as his father signalled to the waiter that he wanted to pay.

Alex suggested that we walk along the beach to Marina del Rey. They wandered ahead, barefoot in the golden sand, and I trailed behind, listening in as they talked.

"People used to mistake me for a tourist during the first couple of years I lived here."

"Let me guess," said Daniel. "Was it your English accent?"

Alex nodded. "Yes, that and my pasty skin. I was working six days a week for my new employer and had no social life, so I never went out."

"You make it sound like it was horrible when you moved here. Was it really that bad?"

"Not at all. My new job offer was a once-in-a-lifetime opportunity. Seeing I had no distractions..."

"You mean Mum and me," Daniel interrupted.

"Danny." Alex stopped walking and turned to his son wearing a pained expression. "That's not what I meant." He walked on. "Because I was all alone here, it meant that whenever I wasn't working, I could channel my energies into building contacts and raising finances until I was confident that I was ready to set up my own company. It took years. Since then, the only times I look back to my previous life are when I think about what you might be doing at that moment and hope that you are healthy and happy."

Daniel padded alongside, his face looking serious as he listened. As we approached the marina and masts came into view, I felt we could have walked for many more miles and the two of them would still be no closer to a reconciliation. For Daniel, though, I could see the irony of being physically present with his father only heightened the pain of the abandonment issues he had suffered during the last twelve years.

"This place is huge," Daniel said.

"I know," Alex said. "I still can't get used to the scale of things over here. Apparently, this marina can hold five thousand boats."

We headed towards the car park. Alex looked around before raising his hand at a figure who was leaning against an expensive-looking sports car. We all walked over.

"Hey, how are you?" said Alex, shaking the man's hand. "This is my son Daniel and his friend Christopher."

"It's a real pleasure to meet you both. I'm Gerry."

His accent was different. I couldn't place it. He was in his late fifties, well built and healthy looking, but with a slight sag around his stomach that his clothing couldn't hide. His smile and handshake were warm, genuine.

"Shall we get going?" he said.

"What's happening?" Daniel asked, mild irritation in his voice.

"It's a surprise," Alex replied.

We followed Gerry along the quayside, passing boats of all types. Fishing vessels were moored next to three-storey craft. Tall yachts bobbed up and down, their sails rolled up and tethered, hulls gleaming, the brasswork's ornate detailing glowing in the sunlight. Gerry stopped at an impressive-looking craft and without hesitating, climbed aboard. He beckoned for us to join him.

"Welcome aboard the *Juanita Mark Two*, named after my second wife."

Alex got on first, and Daniel and I followed.

"What's next, a helicopter ride home?" said Daniel in my ear as we clambered on board. "This is all getting a bit much. I don't like him rubbing my face in everything he has."

I placed my hand on his arm to calm him.

"All he's doing is showing me what he has achieved. I still don't actually know anything about who he is," Daniel continued. "Why is he being like this?"

"Shh," I said in a low voice. "Look. We've only been here a few days. These things take time. He's trying to treat you. Let's just see what happens."

While I agreed with Daniel, I also understood what Alex was trying to do. On the boat, Alex and Gerry busied themselves with checking gauges and fuel lines. Alex came over with some lifebelts. "Gerry works for me at the office, and occasionally we take *Juanita* out for a sail. I thought you two might like it?"

"Brilliant!" I said, not giving Daniel the chance to respond.

"Great! Put these on, and we will head out." He handed us each a belt.

As we left the calm waters of the marina and met the open sea, Gerry increased the engine speed, sending the boat out to meet the first waves. We effortlessly chopped through before hitting deeper waters where the boat settled into a comfortable rhythm with the ocean. After a while, Gerry turned off the engine and locked the helm as he and Alex unfurled the first sail. Together they rapidly rotated winches and spooled out rope. The wind caught the sail, sending ripples across the fabric before pulling it taut. With a surge, we shot forward, our speed increasing. The men deftly set about the second sail, and within a couple of minutes, it was released from captivity, stretched out and straining as the wind filled it from behind. It was thrilling to travel like this at speed with the man I loved. It made us laugh like children.

Chapter Seventeen

The next morning, Alex announced there would be a dinner party at the house that evening. He had to attend to clients who were flying in for a day of meetings. Daniel and I were more than welcome to join them if we wanted to. I wasn't sure, but I didn't want to cause a scene, so I offered to help Alex with the cooking. He looked at me in confusion before explaining that the caterers would be creating all the courses in the main kitchen that afternoon.

"How many people are coming?" I asked Daniel after Alex had left for work.

"Fuck knows," he replied. "This is the first I've heard of it. I just hope the whole evening doesn't revolve around Dad's work."

"Well, I'm guessing it probably will. Do you think we should go?"

"Definitely. I'm not missing out on getting cooked for. Plus, I might get more of a clue about what it is Dad does for a living."

"I don't want to appear out of my depth, surrounded by all these corporate highflyers," I said.

He looked nervous. I remembered his embarrassment from when Anna Hollister had asked him what he did for a living.

"We could make up what we do for work," I said, trying to lift him a little. "I can be a trapeze artist. You can be an astrophysicist or a neurosurgeon."

"This dinner sounds important. We're going to have to be on our best behaviour," he replied, sulking.

"Where's the fun in that?"

* * * *

Alex arrived home at around five, relaxed and in good spirits. He joined us under the pergola, away from the bustle in the kitchen.

"How did it go today?" Daniel asked his father.

"Really well. Most of these people coming tonight are big investors looking to help expand companies. I had to give a couple of presentations and explain how I see my own company growing over the next few years." Alex always became animated whenever he spoke about work. "If they choose to invest in us, then I'll be able to increase R and D even more and double the size of our current facilities. It's all quite exciting," he continued.

"Great," replied his son.

Alex had offered us some of his shirts to wear for the dinner, and once dressed, I didn't feel so nervous. Daniel had chosen an outfit that was remarkably similar to Alex's, and now that the Californian sun was starting to colour Daniel's skin, it was more apparent that they were father and son.

The doorbell sounded, and Alex went to greet the guests, bringing them into the living room. Seven people had arrived, one of whom was Juliette. Everyone spread out, some taking a seat on the sofas, while others stood by the garden. Being typically British, Daniel and I stood together, not even contemplating starting up a conversation with any of the strangers. We felt out of our depth but couldn't avoid it for too long. Juliette appeared in front of us.

"Good evening, boys."

"Good evening, Juliette," we replied in unison, which made us sound like schoolboys answering the teacher. We all laughed, and it broke the ice.

"You both look handsome all dressed up. Last time I saw you, neither of you were wearing very much."

Daniel blushed. I was in awe of her confidence and elegance. She was quite the contrast to some of the other guests, including one man who wore a gaudy yet expensive-looking suit. He was short and rotund, and his stubby fingers boasted numerous chunky gold rings. He had a tan the colour of rust, and his thick drawling accent sounded Texan.

"What do you do at Alex's company?" I asked her, more for the benefit of Daniel, rather than out of genuine interest.

"Well, it's a bit of a story. I studied for my degree in Aeronautical Engineering at ETH Zurich, then did a Master's. Being Swiss, I was hoping to stay there, but I soon heard about some exciting things happening in America. I decided to come here for a one-month trip, and well, now ten years later, here I am still in LA. Alex made me an offer I couldn't refuse."

"Speaking of the devil," I said, as Alex walked up behind her, placing a hand on her waist.

"I hope you're not revealing any company secrets, Juliette," he said.

"I was telling the boys how you practically begged me to come and work for you."

"I don't know what I'd do without you," he said into her ear.

Daniel was not impressed, but before he had a chance to react, his father pulled Juliette away and back towards the investors. Her charm was clearly needed.

"They definitely have some sort of history," said Daniel.

I nodded, reluctant to say too much. Speculation could be just as damaging as outright accusation. These were other people's private lives, people I had just met.

We stood by the open door to the garden, watching as people mingled, then separated and moved on to talk to someone else. It was hypnotic to watch, accompanied by the heady sweet smell of jasmine drifting in from outside.

"Maybe we should have worn black trousers and a white shirt. That way we could have blended in with the waiting staff."

I turned to see where Daniel was pointing — a waiter stood patiently with a tray of drinks, while a couple of others circled unobtrusively with canapés.

Laughter erupted from a corner of the room, where a cluster of men were stood. Alex disentangled himself from the group and hurried over towards us.

"Daniel, there some people I'd like to introduce you to." He put his arm around Daniel's shoulder and started to guide him away.

Daniel looked back at me, and Alex followed his gaze.

"It's just for a minute," Alex said. "I'm sure Christopher will be fine."

Two women were sitting on a nearby sofa talking softly to each other.

Alex paused beside them. "Ladies, have you been introduced to Christopher yet? He's from England."

The women looked up at me expectantly as Alex ushered Daniel away. I stood there, my mouth opening and closing like a goldfish, not knowing what to say.

"Could I get you ladies a drink? A glass of champagne perhaps?" They both nodded and smiled, so I moved away with relief, thankful for my new role as a member of the waiting staff.

I plucked two delicate flutes from the tray of a passing waiter and returned them to the women, then excused myself, not wanting to engage in any banal conversation.

By the door to the garden, I had a perfect vantage point of the whole room and watched as Alex introduced Daniel to the group of men, who welcomed him into their enclave with handshakes and backslapping. I gritted my teeth as he was swallowed up.

"You look lost without him," observed Juliette, appearing by my side out of nowhere.

I gave her a tight-lipped smile and said nothing. Close up, I couldn't help but admire how flawless she was.

"Alex is a very proud father, you know. Having Daniel here after all those years is extremely important to him."

I nodded. "I'm sure he missed Daniel very much. It's all quite sad."

"Alex has never been one to wear his heart on his sleeve, but there hasn't been a week that's gone by when he hasn't referred to him in some way. I guess they have a lot of catching up to do."

I watched Juliette appraise the group of men. Her face was devoid of emotion.

"Is he a tough boss to work for?"

She turned to me and her expression softened a little. "Not at all. He has high expectations and standards but is so passionate about his work that all his employees want to give him their best."

We both sipped our drinks. Her gaze never left the group of men in the corner.

"Don't you miss Europe?" I asked, genuinely intrigued.

"Of course. Especially my family and friends. I go back every couple of years, but it's not the same. I've worked really hard to get where I am now and given up so much. It's a tough business and very male dominated."

Her gaze was now focused on Daniel, who was standing listening as a man talked to him animatedly. For someone who was normally quiet and relatively shy, he seemed to be holding his own.

"How long are you staying with Alex?" she asked.

"Oh, only a couple of weeks. Then we fly back home. We both have jobs to go back to."

"That's a shame. You must come again," Juliette said, and clinked her glass against mine, the creases of a smile forming at the corners of her lips.

Eventually we were summoned to the dining room by Alex. Two huge floral arrangements stood either side of an ice sculpture that formed the centrepiece of the table. I felt like I was attending a state banquet.

Daniel was sitting opposite me, and together we somehow managed to navigate our way through the social etiquette required to get through an occasion like this. It helped that his foot caressed my ankles throughout. The food was exquisite, each and every course. When it was over and the guests were about to leave, I was relieved to have enjoyed the evening. There had been a lot of wealth and power at the table, but I didn't once feel small or out of place, despite expecting the worst.

Chapter Eighteen

We were starting to get used to Alex springing surprise plans upon us, and that weekend he told us we would all be going to Laguna Beach to stay at the home of his friend, the artist Luis Batista. I had endured yet another interrupted night's sleep and wasn't up to socialising. I had once more crept into the lounge with my book as Daniel slept, but I couldn't concentrate. I wanted to be by myself. Something was bugging me. It had come out of a dream but was based on something real. A reflection of Alex in the rear-view mirror of his car was playing on my mind — his smile as he put on his sunglasses. That smile, there was a trace of something in it. It wasn't pride — he was hiding something. Whatever it was, that smile was betraying something true. I decided to go back to bed, to return to Daniel. I lay there for a while like a voyeur, watching him sleep until I drifted off again.

On the drive down, I managed to rest a little, but it left me feeling groggy by the time we turned off the freeway and onto Laguna Canyon Road. Daniel, however, was well rested and was in his element, completely at home in these new surroundings. We descended towards the coast. The slopes on either side of us were dotted with colourful houses that were angled towards the ocean. I glimpsed dashes of Etruscan orange and cobalt blue through the trees. The bottom of the canyon opened out onto a beautiful vista of golden sand and rolling surf. Alex drove us along some residential streets until we pulled up outside a picture-perfect China-blue-painted house with an immaculately tended front garden. Alex hadn't told us much about his friend, but I was taken aback when I saw just how beautiful he was, tall and slim with honey-coloured skin, and his face was grooved with lines that showed he laughed often. He wore faded blue jeans and a shirt splattered with paints of every colour.

A huge collection of artwork lined the walls of his home — images rendered in ink, watercolour, oil and pastel, some in ostentatious gilt frames, others boxed in by the clean thin lines of black or beech-coloured wood. A postcard-sized pencil sketch of a tree nestled next to a three-foot-square explosion of red, an amorphous image of such randomness that only when I looked closely could I see the subtle lightening and darkening of the hues. It was clear Luis was the artist who had created much of the art in Alex's home. The indiscriminate nature of the artworks' subjects and their chaotic positioning on the walls made me want to study the pictures in more detail.

The kitchen was in comfortable disarray, very much in contrast to Alex's minimalist kitchen with its steel and marble. The floor was layered with old, bleached floorboards that creaked when stepped on. The walls had been painted with different washes of yellow, the shades swirling together like custard in a bowl.

"Let's go and see Jonas," Luis said. "He's in the garden. Then I'll get us some drinks."

Luis explained that Jonas was his latest protégé. He had been working with him on an exhibition that was due to open later in the year. There was no grass in the garden. Instead, the space was laid out with small square tiles that circled the base of an old eucalyptus tree. Beneath the tree, sitting at a table, was a figure in his early twenties, with light brown skin and a shock of tight ringlets framing his handsome face.

"Jonas is studying fine art here in Laguna," Luis said. "He's just had his first exhibition as part of the festival."

"Did it go well?" asked Alex.

"Everything sold," replied Jonas. I knew if I was to see him walking, he would swagger.

"Are you from around here?" said Alex.

"Yes, I've lived in LA all my life. I study here during the week, and I rent a place down near the boardwalk. I go back to see my parents most weekends. They live in Encino."

"Oh, that's just down the road from me," said Alex. "I live in Calabasas."

Jonas was looking at Daniel. "I'll have to drop by some time," he replied with sudden enthusiasm.

He left the words hanging in the air. I looked around the table, but no one else seemed to pick up on his thinly veiled flirtation. Luis brought out a tray of margaritas and the conversation began to flow. After a while, I began to relax, even though Jonas had zeroed in on Daniel and shut me out.

Luis, however, was gracious enough to make me feel welcome, and when I told him I worked in a bookshop, he invited me into the house to look at his library. I was glad to leave Jonas under the eucalyptus tree but was worried he might start something up with Daniel. Would he dare with Alex around? Luis led me into a room that was packed from floor to ceiling with books on three of its walls. Rich leather-bound tomes and large expensive-looking publications were stacked, filling row upon row of shelves. There were thousands. I traced my fingers across the volumes. There were so many authors I didn't recognise, despite all my years in the bookshop. Then I saw a well-thumbed paperback edition of *The Swimming-Pool Library* and remembered how much Daniel had enjoyed it when he'd read my copy.

There were sculptures scattered about the room on plinths — male heads in bronze, fired clay and carved wood.

"Did you make these?"

"Yes, all of them."

"Don't you find it unnerving being in here alone at night with them all watching?"

"I enjoy their company. I know all the models in the flesh."

I was envious of his creativity and connection. I also admired his perfect diction and intelligence. I took in his frame as he opened the connecting door. Did I want him to look at me, too?

"Let's go to my studio…"

There was something about him that seemed familiar, yet I couldn't quite place it. He was very gentle in his movements and softly spoken. There was an attraction on my part, and I didn't know why.

Beyond the door was a kiln and pottery wheel, while the far wall brimmed with glazed pottery and figurines displayed neatly on shelves. Playful caricatures of animals sat alongside naked male figures, some crudely carved, others finely detailed. There was even more artwork, charcoal sketches next to other pieces that were finished and framed. Long strips of framing hung on the wall above.

"You make your own frames?"

"Yes," he replied. "The frame is as important as the art itself. You can ruin a piece if you do not consider what encapsulates it. I like to experiment."

He held my gaze for a second, and I didn't look away.

I scanned the easels in the middle of the room, hoping to glimpse something secret. One featured vivid blocks of colour in the same style as the pictures I'd seen in Alex's house.

"You must be proud of your talent," I said.

He offered me a warm smile.

"Oh, there you are!" Alex strolled into the studio. "I wondered where you were. What are you up to?"

I was startled, unsure of what to say.

"I came in to see if you were all right. You've been gone a while. Christopher, I just need a word with Luis, if you don't mind."

"Yes, I should go back," I said, aware of the heat in my face. I didn't wait for a response and left them both standing in Luis' studio.

I could hear laughter as I approached the garden. Jonas was sitting close to Daniel — he was practically in his lap. Whatever it was they were discussing, they both found it amusing. I rested a hand on Daniel's shoulder.

"Where have you been, then? You've been a while."

"Luis just showed me his library and studio."

Jonas let out a small scoff.

"Just been hearing about Jonas' apartment here in Laguna," Daniel said. "It overlooks the sea, no less."

I could tell Daniel was getting a little tipsy. The way he was so easily impressed reminded me of the American tourists who came into the bookshop back in Bath, taking pictures and commenting on how "quaint" everything was. He turned back to Jonas.

"You should see where we are staying in Calabasas. It's pretty amazing."

"I'll show you mine if you show me yours?"

Daniel laughed. He swayed in his seat. The alcohol and heat of the sun had reddened his cheeks. He stretched out in the chair and closed his eyes, his long legs reaching far under the table, his arms behind his head.

"Imagine living somewhere like this where you are so close to the beach and it's sunny every day?" he said. He opened one eye and cocked his head towards me.

"It would be pretty perfect, I guess." I couldn't deny it. "Although the novelty would soon fade, I'm sure."

"Well, it beats those cold winters back home. Here you could wear shorts on Christmas Day."

"I kind of like the seasons back home," I said sharply.

He kept his eyes closed as sunlight bathed his face through the gaps in the branches overhead. Jonas made no attempt to hide his gaze.

Eventually, Alex and Luis emerged from the library and crossed the garden to join us. The afternoon glided comfortably by. Enhanced by crisp chilled white wine, Luis proved to be a natural storyteller, and after some prompting, he explained to us how he had tiptoed onto the art scene after he had graduated, and now many years later, his work sold internationally. He didn't brag as he recounted his story and was more self-effacing. It made him all the more likeable and attractive.

Luis suggested a stroll down to the boardwalk. It felt good to see the ocean again. The sun hung low, bathing us in a haze of yellow bronzed ochre. We sat on some benches by the beach to admire the view, and I managed to get Daniel to myself for the first time that day.

"Thank you for coming with me to visit Dad," he said. "Having no one to share this with would have made for a somewhat lonely experience... It's all a bit surreal."

He briefly rested his head on my shoulder, and I glanced at the others on their nearby bench. I didn't want to be caught, but no one had noticed. The beach was still busy with people. Jonas came over to say goodbye, saying he had work to do, and pointed out his duplex across the street. I wasn't sad to see him go but experienced a flash of irritation while Daniel watched his retreating figure. We went back to join Alex and Luis, who were talking about Jonas.

"He can act a bit spoilt at times," Luis confessed. "He's used to getting what he wants."

"He'll go far in the art world, then," countered Alex.

Back at the house, we spent the evening under the eucalyptus tree. I was far more relaxed without Jonas hovering over Daniel. The sea air and alcohol had made us gloriously tired, and we were yawning plenty by the time Luis showed us to our rooms. He pointed out a bathroom and separate bedrooms for Alex, Daniel and me. Once we were sure Luis had gone downstairs, we brushed our teeth together and both went to my room. Daniel moulded his body comfortably around mine and fell asleep. I listened as his breathing slowed, wishing I could sleep as easily. With the heat of the day gone, the house settled. I heard the muted murmur of traffic in the distance, the groan of pipes and the creaking of floorboards in the corridor outside our door. I eventually drifted off in Daniel's embrace.

* * * *

We both woke late, and by the time we came downstairs, breakfast was waiting for us in the kitchen with a note telling us to help ourselves. We took croissants, fruit, coffee and orange juice into the garden.

"This reminds me of your breakfasts back home," Daniel said to me.

"Yes, but without the cloudless skies and scent of the ocean."

I liked that we had a shared ritual that was ours alone. We ate slowly, and when we were done, we took the breakfast things back to the kitchen.

"I wonder where they've gone?" said Daniel, setting a tray down.

I shrugged.

"I'm just going to grab my sunscreen, back in a sec." He brushed his hand against my thighs as he left. For a second, I imagined this was our kitchen.

I hummed to myself as I rinsed the orange juice glasses, too nervous to put them in the dishwasher. I was nearly done when footsteps thundered down the stairs. There was then a distinct slam of a door. A minute later, I heard softer slower footsteps on the stairs. Luis walked into the room, looking troubled.

"Have you seen Daniel?"

"No, he went to get sun cream."

"Damn. I think that must have been him leaving the house."

"Why would he do that? What happened?"

He looked uncomfortable. "Alex and I were upstairs, getting changed."

"And?"

He ignored me and said, "One of us needs to find Daniel."

"I'll go."

I went to the front door and stepped out into the blazing sunshine. The heat of the day was already rising fast. I strode to the pavement and scanned the street. There was no one to be seen. I then thought of where he might be.

I tried to remember the route, walking until the road opened up onto the South Coast highway. Opposite there were hotels and shops, with the sea behind them, all familiar from our walk yesterday. I crossed to the ocean side of the street and looked for gaps between the buildings that would lead me to the beach behind. I followed a weed-covered path down onto the golden sand. People were carefree, lying on towels or playing in the surf. I looked up and down the beach helplessly, scanning their faces. I felt the pull to go right, towards a park farther up the beach. As I trudged along the sand, I wondered what had happened.

I walked for a few minutes until I reached the grass. It was set back from the sand by the curved boardwalk. I walked along its serpentine length, studying the folk who sat on benches. I then spotted Daniel's outline on a bench, gazing out to sea. He was in the same position as when I had first seen him, elbows resting on his knees, chin cupped in his hands. I sat beside him. Neither of us spoke for a while, instead watching a few distant surfers riding waves until they tumbled into the sea.

"I saw something I shouldn't have," he said eventually. "I walked past Luis' bedroom. The door was open. They stepped apart, pretending nothing had happened, but I know what I saw." The muscles in his jaw clenched.

I remained wordless, a little shocked, truth be told. There had been an air of familiarity about Luis when he invited me to look at his library and studio. I had seen it before with older gay friends. They had the same quiet confidence of men in happy acceptance of their sexuality. However, if Alex was gay, then he might not have come out yet. The drama was far from over.

"C'mon. Let's walk a bit," I said, standing.

"Do you think I should confront my dad about what I saw?"

"Confront? To be honest, I don't think any confrontation is a good thing."

He looked sullen and in the mood for a fight. I moved closer and tried to soothe him.

"Listen. Whatever you saw," I continued, "there has to be a reason why they haven't said anything. Remember, we haven't told them about us yet."

He glanced at me. I could tell then, that in the heat of the moment he had forgotten about telling *anyone* we were a couple. We were just as guilty.

"Let's go back. Luis has gone to a lot of trouble for us this weekend. Maybe this was your dad's way of introducing you to Luis, before he was ready to tell you that they're a couple?"

He breathed out slowly. "Look. I know you're right. That doesn't make *it* right, though."

"So it's okay for you to be gay, but not him…?"

He stopped.

"Sorry," I said, but knowing he was acting a little spoilt. "That was uncalled for." He continued to walk, and I felt a little relieved.

"Don't worry. I promise I'll behave," he said. "But don't expect me to be the life and soul of the party. Let's get through this, so we can get out of here."

* * * *

When we arrived at the house, we went straight to the back garden to find Alex and Luis, but unfortunately Jonas was there, too. I gritted my teeth as once again his gaze lingered over Daniel, his long lashes almost caressing his body. I took some comfort in the fact Daniel hadn't noticed. He was far too distracted. As we approached the table, I said a silent prayer to whatever gay God there was above and hoped for the best.

We must have been gone a while, because the table was set, all ready for lunch to be served. I took a swig of beer and tried to gauge the atmosphere. It was mixed, to say the least, even with Luis' attempts at levity. Alex was also drinking beer, talking to Jonas about his recent exhibition, although he was clearly distracted. He kept stealing glances at his son, who was now looking at everyone except his dad.

Luis asked for my help in the kitchen. I gladly left the table and followed him inside. In the kitchen, he leant back against the sink. "I guess Daniel told you what he saw?"

I didn't say anything either way but let him continue.

"Can I trust you?" he said.

I nodded.

"Do not tell Daniel..."

As soon as he said this, I felt like asking him not to divulge, but my curiosity was too strong.

"As I'm sure you have both worked out, Alex and I are together."

"That's fine with me," I replied. We both laughed, and his shoulders relaxed a little.

"Alex is so fucking goddamn English, though. No offence."

"None taken."

"He's so private and can't come to terms with the fact he's in a relationship, let alone a gay one. If he had his way, no one would ever know. I told him that when I came out many, many years ago, the world didn't stop turning. He needs to understand that life moves on. This will do him some good in the long term, but of course he won't see that now."

Luis opened the oven door, and after donning a battered pair of oven gloves, he removed three large trays of food. The smell was divine.

"Here, take one of these outside and then come back for the next. And while you're at it, let me know what's going on out there."

I took the gloves and carried the tray of meat down to the table. Alex and Jonas were still talking, while Daniel was looking off into the middle distance, blanking everything out. They barely noticed me sliding the tray onto the table. I went back to the kitchen where Luis was straining brightly coloured vegetables in the sink.

"Talking of repressed Englishmen," he said, "why do I have the feeling there's something you haven't told me, either?"

I didn't want this to be the moment, especially without Daniel here.

"Suddenly got shy, Christopher?" came a voice from behind me. Luis threw Jonas a dark glance.

"Yes, it's true. Daniel and I are together."

"I know," said Luis without looking up from the sink. "I knew it the moment you both walked in. You English sure love to keep secrets."

"Daniel didn't want to tell Alex straight away until he could be sure of his reaction."

"Well, I expect that's one hell of a conversation they're going to have," said Jonas with a drawl.

Luis threw the oven gloves at him, and he caught them deftly. Luis then pointed at a hot ceramic pot, steam rising from inside. "Take that to the table. We'll be with you in a minute."

Jonas scowled, clearly not wanting to miss more gossip. I hoped he wouldn't say anything over lunch. Once he was no longer in earshot, Luis said, "The best we can do is support them. They need to sort it out between themselves, without any interference."

He leant forward and hugged me. I hadn't realised how much I needed it.

* * * *

After the meal, which was a pantomime of British civility with very few words exchanged, Alex announced we had to drive back to Calabasas, as he had to work early the next morning. Even Luis looked relieved.

As we said our goodbyes, Luis shook my hand. "I hope to see you again before your holiday is over," he said with genuine warmth. I felt the connection and was grateful for it. I begrudgingly turned to Jonas, gritting my teeth as he hugged Daniel.

"I'm looking after my parents' place next week while they're away in San Francisco so maybe I'll come by and say hi," he said to him.

"You would be most welcome," replied Alex on his behalf. "Maybe we could see some of your artwork, too?"

"Sure, why don't you come to my exhibition instead? It's moving from Laguna to a gallery in downtown LA next Friday." I couldn't be sure whether a glimmer of excitement crossed Daniel's face.

I went to take my usual seat at the back of the car, but Daniel brushed past and slipped in before me. "You sit up front," he commanded.

Alex flinched but said nothing. All the way back, the radio played just that little bit louder. I turned once to glance at Daniel, who was sitting directly behind Alex, hidden from the rear-view mirror. His eyes gave nothing away.

Chapter Nineteen

When we had gotten back to the house in the late afternoon, Daniel had gone to our room and stayed there for the entire evening. Alex was nowhere to be seen. I sat by the pool, uncomfortable and wishing I was anywhere but here. The next morning, by the time we were up, Alex had already left for work. Daniel headed straight to the pool, swimming laps with furious intensity. The angry wake he left behind reminded me of the sepia paddle steamer photo on my sitting-room wall. I missed my flat and Ptolemy. I liked my simple life without its dramas. Although I now knew I loved Daniel, I still didn't know that much about him. After seeing the change in his personality since we had arrived in LA, part of me was worried that I was about to lose that person I had first fallen in love with.

It became clear that today was going to be another day spent by the pool. I didn't mind, especially after the drama of yesterday. It was good to feel the sun on my skin, and I had books to read. What stung, though, was just how introspective Daniel had become. He was cordial and said "thank you" when I placed food and drink next to him, but he didn't engage with me at all. I tried to empathise and put myself in his shoes. If that had happened to my father, how would I have reacted? It reminded me of a dark period with my parents when I was younger. I quickly closed the door on the memory, unwilling to think about it further.

It was early afternoon when Daniel announced he was tired after his swim and was going for a nap. There was no invitation for me to join him. As he walked towards the guest cottage, he glanced over, as if taunting me to challenge him. He had woken up ready for a fight, and it didn't matter who with. His expression was solid and unflinching. I was seeing another side of him. As he disappeared through the cottage doors, I thought of the saying, "You always hurt the ones you love," but I was starting to question if I was even loved.

I went over scenes at the flat in Bath — kisses on the sofa, caresses as we cooked and the constant need to touch each other. Proclamations of love, though? I loved him, but I hadn't told him that. I had crossed a bridge into a new land and now realised I had given myself to him completely. I couldn't say that he had done the same. He was too reserved for that. If he rejected me now, I would be lost. More lost than I felt now? Fuck, what was happening to me?

My bag was by the pool, alongside one of my books. It had my wallet and money inside. I was dressed. I didn't have to stay here. I could go anywhere. Was I just meant to sit and wait for him to wake up? I grabbed my bag and headed towards the main house. I was being impulsive. It unnerved and exhilarated me in equal measure. I didn't know where I was going. All I knew was I wanted to get out of this suffocating house.

Outside on the quiet tree-lined street, not a car could be heard. There were no pedestrians either. I looked behind me at the house. I could go back, pretend nothing had happened and that today was idyllic, creep into the cottage and undress, then nestle up to Daniel as he slumbered away the afternoon, waking up entwined in his arms. Was that what would happen? I imagined this romantic picture, but in reality, Daniel would be lying on one side, immune and oblivious to my presence, my proximity unwelcome. He needed space. And why was I out here if I didn't crave it, too? I breathed in deeply and walked along the street, not quite knowing where I was going. It felt good to be setting off alone.

There was a scent of jasmine and honeysuckle in the air, which calmed me. At the end of the road was a busy intersection. I stood there for a few minutes, uncertain about what to do next. A taxi approached, and on a wild impulse, I flagged it down, not really expecting it to stop. I felt relieved as it cruised past me, but then the brake lights illuminated. I walked towards it and opened the door, "Could you take me downtown please?" I said, trying to sound as if I had done this a million times before, but aware that my accent and body language might instantly give me away as a tourist.

I thought about how much I had in my wallet and hoped the driver wouldn't stiff me. I sank into the seat, taking in the cloying scent of the synthetic air freshener dangling from the rear-view mirror. I suddenly thought about the tranquillity of Alex's pool, and I almost asked the driver to turn back. But, no, I needed this. Time out.

I ran my fingers through my hair and let out a deep sigh.

"Bad day, huh?"

"Sorry?" I answered.

"You look like you need a break."

I laughed. "That bad, am I? Actually, I'm already here on a break. And I'm good, thanks. How can things not be good when you're in LA?"

The driver scoffed. "Not everywhere here looks as good as it does in the movies. Believe me, I've seen a lot."

To him, I was just another dumb tourist, and for once I agreed with him.

He dropped me off in the middle of downtown and I stepped out into the heat of the day. I took in the buildings, the honking traffic and the constant stream of people from all directions. It was an eclectic crowd, and it felt good to be among them. No wonder Daniel could see the allure. I wandered the wide pavements, experiencing sensory overload, but for once I didn't mind. Even though we had been out with Alex and seen the sights, this was more visceral and exciting. For a short while, I wanted to see as much as I could by myself. It was liberating to wander, not knowing what was around the corner.

Normally I would have been anxious about getting lost, but there were so many taxis in the unending traffic that I felt more confident. The mood downtown was infectious, and I began to feel alive. I walked down a road. The central row of palm trees stretched off into the distance. I took a couple of turns and soon came to Grand Park. It was strange to find this open, leafy retreat nestled among the streets lined with buildings. It wasn't as traditional as an English park. It was minimalist and modern. I drew level with a group of people stretched out on mats. I thought they were doing yoga. There was balletic beauty in their collective movement. Ahead, a fountain shot graceful arcs of water high into the air, rainbows appearing in the haze. Beyond the fountain were some seats in the shade of the trees.

I sat for a while taking it all in. On my left was a woman, barefoot, wearing a diaphanous white dress, her legs wrapped around a cello. As she played, the music reminded me of the bookshop in Bath and the quiet meditative time I spent replenishing the shelves. I felt homesick. I wished I had a book with me, just so I could pass the time thinking about imaginary lives, rather than my own. I was a little relieved when I spotted some other tourists. They were wandering slowly, smiling as they took pictures and scanned their guidebooks.

I spied one man sitting nearby on a single chair by a café. He had sandy-coloured hair and was as beautiful as Daniel. He was reading something, a novel or a guidebook, I couldn't tell. I knew I judged people by what they read. Call it habit, but Art was guilty of it, too. This man was sitting side on, so I could only see half his profile. Another older man was sitting next to him but facing the opposite direction, also reading. I guessed him to be in his early fifties. Because their chairs were almost side by side, like a loveseat, they could freely converse. Despite the fact they both had books, they were still talking to each other. I imagined they might be a couple. They looked at peace, knowing the other was there.

I thought of the couples I knew. Ben and Tabitha…their relationship thrived on its volatility. Ben's meekness incensed Tabitha, and her strength of character weakened him. Alex and Luis…Alex repressed and English, Luis passionate and open. Who was I to judge? I had no idea, really.

I didn't remember my parents laughing together or embracing each other. Maybe there was the occasional arm around the shoulder for the sake of a holiday snap, but that was it. But I still knew they loved each other. My memory was sometimes hazy when it came to my childhood, but there had been arguments. My father had stormed out of the house once, returning several hours later and going straight upstairs. I had peeked in through the bedroom door to see him flat out on the marital bed. It was clear to me now that he had been drinking.

A rattling sound came from somewhere over to my left. A woman was pushing a small shopping cart towards the fountain. She was talking to herself and laughing. She sat down on a nearby seat and kicked off her sandals. I watched as she removed her bright bandana, letting a mass of tight black curls fall. She then stood up again and went to the fountain, reaching over to let the jets of water soak the colourful fabric. She pressed the cloth to her face and neck. Her ragged cart was filled with rubbish. I thought of Maggie back in Bath and how she often slept on the street down from the bookshop.

The line of the shadows had lengthened. I wasn't sure how long I had been here, but I knew it was time to go. I was thirsty, too. I went to the small café and bought a bottle of water, deliberately passing close to the couple on their makeshift loveseat as I made my way out. The woman with the sodden fabric was now sitting in my seat. I went to her and held out the bottle of water.

"I have this spare, if you want it? It will just go to waste if not," I said through dry lips.

She took it from me immediately, and said, "Good to see there's still some gentlemen roun' here."

I nodded once and walked on.

When I returned to Alex's, Daniel was sitting near the pool, his posture rigid on the chair. His head whipped round.

"Where have you been?" he said in an accusatory manner.

I bristled. He was wearing a pristine pair of white cotton trousers and an aquamarine linen shirt I hadn't seen before. He looked as if he had been born here. His suntan made him more handsome than ever. I was no match for him, no matter how hard I tried — I couldn't compete with this new life that was more or less his for the taking. How could he even consider me an option?

"I went for a walk."

"Oh."

"I like your shirt," I said, keen to change the subject. "Where did you get it?"

He flashed me an irritable glance. "It was a gift from Jonas."

I held my hands up in surrender. "Well, it looks great..."

He turned to face the house, and I went to the guest cottage, needing to wash the grime of the city off my face and hands, as well as the thought of Jonas giving my boyfriend such a beautiful gift. I knew Daniel was waiting for his father to come home.

Eventually, Alex came down the stairs. He looked tired. I went to greet him. "Hi, how was work? You must be tired. Let me fetch you a beer. Do you fancy eating out again tonight, or get a takeaway, if you have those around here? My treat." I was babbling wildly. All I wanted to do was defuse a potentially volatile situation. Alex looked flustered.

"Sorry, what? Work? Oh, it was fine. Eat out? Erm... I don't mind. Whatever. Yes, a beer would be good, actually."

Without thinking, I went to grab the beers, leaving father and son alone. By the time I had returned, the show had begun, and Daniel was standing over a seated Alex, screaming at him.

"So when were you thinking of explaining to me what the fuck all that was about yesterday? I bet you all had a great laugh at my expense. Stupid Daniel is the last to know his dad is a fag. Who else knew? Jonas?"

My breath caught in my throat as I waited for Alex to react to the homophobic slur Daniel had just branded him with. All he gave, though, was a barely perceptible nod in reply.

"How about you, Christopher?" asked Daniel, as I placed the beer bottles on the table.

"No, of course not. I didn't know." I put up my hands to ward off his glare. I'd never seen Daniel so angry before.

He regarded me for a moment before he turned back to his father. "One of the reasons I wanted to visit was to tell you something incredibly important, but instead, once more you turn out to be the fucking centre of attention in my pathetic little life. I was going to sit you down and explain that I've changed from that poor kid you last saw all those years ago. I wanted you to know how happy I am. I'm gay, too, you know."

"I know. We saw that straightaway—" Alex began.

"Unbelievable," Daniel interrupted. He raised his arms in the air, then let them collapse to his sides.

"Look, son..." Alex attempted to rise from his seat but sank back down as Daniel talked over him.

"Why couldn't you have just told me when we arrived? Instead, you take us to meet your *friend*, where

I happened to catch you and Luis hiding upstairs like a couple of horny teenagers."

"I tried, but there never seemed to be the right time," explained Alex, looking more and more uncomfortable.

"Just like you never found the right time to spend with Mum and me," Daniel fired back.

I flinched. It was a cheap shot, words intended to wound. Judging by the expression on Alex's face, they had found their mark. Silence fell under the pergola. Of course Daniel had every right to be angry. It must have been a shock finding them upstairs together like that, but we had been clandestine, too, a fact that he had conveniently forgotten again. It was clear to me now, though, that this was not about sexuality and secrets, but the pain of abandonment, something I knew all about. The difference was that my parents hadn't chosen to leave me behind, but Alex had. That had to hurt.

"What can I do to make things better? I can't change the past. What do you want to know?" asked Alex.

"The truth." Daniel crossed his arms and waited.

Alex exhaled slowly, meeting his son's hostile gaze. "Okay, like what?"

"How long have you been seeing Luis? Are you an item? Was Luis the reason you left Mum?"

"No, no, he wasn't. I didn't leave her for anyone but myself. I met Luis six years ago at a cookery class. He was renting an apartment in Pasadena, not too far from where I was living at the time, but then he moved down to Laguna Beach. I used to drive down to see him, and we would cook together. He knew I had been married and had a son, but if it was late, he would let me stay the night, and over time we grew closer. We're not officially a couple, but I guess you could say we are together." Alex looked uneasy revealing his personal history with Luis. I guessed that since the breakup of his marriage, Alex hadn't had to explain himself to anybody for a long time.

"Well, *Dad*, I'm happy for you. All these years away, and I was worried about what you would think and whether you would disown me or hate me, and then all along, you were living a lie, being someone you were not in your sham of a marriage. It seems to me you've breezed into this new life of yours without even a backwards glance. If only you knew the things I've had to endure to discover who I am. Do you know what? I'm out of here. I need some time out. This is all too fucked up." Without another word, Daniel strode through the open doorway back into the lounge area and disappeared up the stairs towards the kitchen.

Both Alex and I stood at the same time as Daniel left the table. "Where are you going now?" I called, irate. Alex stood frozen in a moment of indecision, before swearing under his breath and following Daniel. I left them both to it. I was exhausted.

I stayed in my chair and focused on the soft drone of the insects that rested amid the jasmine on the pergola roof. A few minutes turned into ten, and after half an hour, I ventured into the main house. It was quiet—not even the air-con stirred. I went to the front of the house and looked out of a window. Alex's car was gone, and another hour passed before he returned.

"He's done it again," he said. "Bloody stormed off. I've just spent an hour driving around the neighbourhood, and he's nowhere to be found. Where the hell do you think he's gone?"

"I've no idea, Alex. I don't know this area at all."

"Well, you're his bloody boyfriend. You should know. After all, you've been fucking him under my roof since you got here."

I sprang up from my seat and moved away from him. "Are you kidding? I've done nothing wrong. If anything, he's the one who has been crying out for help since you abandoned him."

"Abandoned him? I left all my contact details with my ex. I thought he wanted nothing to do with me."

"I lost both my parents a few years ago, and I still miss them every day. They're never coming back. Daniel's felt abandoned by you for the past twelve years, yet you're still alive and can do something about it. You could have tried harder if you wanted to."

"What the fuck was I meant to do? Joanna made things bloody difficult at times."

I didn't answer, because I didn't know. I realised how little Daniel had told me about his past, even though it seemed as if he'd told me a lot. Inside I felt hurt. Daniel had walked out and left me, too.

"I just hope he doesn't do anything stupid," I said.

"What do you mean?"

It had been just a thought, spoken out loud. I recalled Daniel telling me about his decline after he was assaulted by Hector.

"What are you not telling me about *my* son?"

"All I can say is that he's been in some dark places. I don't think you realise what he's been through. He appears resilient, but he's fragile."

"Is he in danger of harming himself?"

"I don't know. I don't think so…"

"You don't think so?" Alex scoffed. "You're supposed to be his boyfriend."

I could feel myself getting hotter. "That's not fair. I've never seen him act like this before. He's angry at you, not me, remember? You haven't told him anything, including why you left so suddenly. Was it *really* the job offer over here, or was there another reason?"

"It's none of your business," he said flatly.

"That might be so, but you definitely owe Daniel an explanation."

"Don't tell me what I should say to my son, Christopher."

He went back into the house, leaving me alone and powerless to do anything. Daniel was gone, and I was sitting in paradise, wholly dejected.

I woke up alone at two a.m. The bedsheets were rumpled and twisted. I had tried to sleep on Daniel's side, but the bed was far too big for one person. I went into the kitchen and noticed some paper had been pushed under the front door. It was a note from Alex with the number of his office, asking me to call if Daniel turned up the following day.

* * * *

When I awoke, the light in the room was bright. I wasn't alone in the room.

As I stirred, Daniel came over. "I'm sorry," he whispered.

The relief was immediate. "Thank God. I was so worried. Where did you go?"

"I went out walking. I needed to clear my head."

"All night?" I pressed.

"No. I stayed with Jonas. He gave me his parents' address and number when we were at Luis' place..."

"I see," I replied, keeping the tone of my voice neutral, not wanting to betray the turmoil churning inside of me.

"Nothing happened," he added hastily, sitting on the side of the bed. "I just wanted to be away from this fucking house and my dad. I crashed on a sofa."

"I understand you need space from your dad, but..." My voice trailed off. I couldn't find the right words. Did he realise how much his leaving had hurt me?

Daniel looked up at me, then away. "I just needed to get out of here. I was feeling suffocated."

Was I to blame for that, too, or was I being overly sensitive, analysing his every word for hidden meaning? "Have you seen your dad yet?" I asked instead, sitting up and smothering the questioning voice in my head.

"No, he would have left for work hours ago."

He unbuttoned his shirt and stepped out of his trousers and underwear.

"I'm taking a shower," he said.

"Fine." I wondered what he wanted to wash away.

Daniel padded naked into the bathroom, stopping only to grab a towel from the back of the bedroom door. I swung my legs out of bed and stood. Alex's note was face down on the bedside table. I was torn with indecision about what to do next. The logical step was to phone Alex, but would that lead to yet another confrontation between them both? Water hissed as the shower was turned on. I took a step towards the bathroom. If I could just reason with Daniel and tell him that I understood his pain, would that help to diffuse his deep-seated anger? I moved across to the doorway, which he'd left open.

Daniel stood under the spray with his eyes closed, indistinct, shrouded in a cloud of steam. He was massaging shampoo into his hair. The white creamy lather cascaded down his body, sliding over the contours of his chest. It slowed, as it caught in the blond thatch of his pubic hair, before suggestively flowing in a stream from the end of his penis. My own cock twitched as I stood rooted to the spot, mesmerised. Daniel opened his eyes and saw me standing there. I swallowed hard as desire coursed through my body, igniting a fire in my groin. He regarded me for a long moment, neither of us saying a word, then he abruptly turned his back on me, breaking the spell.

I went to the main house, taking Alex's note with me, and called him. He wasn't available, so I left a message with his assistant, but within an hour he was home.

Daniel was taken aback to see his father step out unannounced onto the patio and walk over to join us where we were sitting by the pool.

"We should talk," Alex said to him. "Where did you go last night?"

"I walked around for ages, and then called a taxi and went to Jonas' parents' house. I needed a break. I slept on the sofa."

"I'm sorry you felt the need to leave, but you have to stop thinking of me as some sort of monster," Alex said. "I'm also capable of making mistakes, just like anybody. You know full well being gay is not a lifestyle choice. But for me, growing up, well, things were very different, so cut me some slack here."

"Okay…" Before Daniel could say anything more, Alex overrode him.

"Look. I grew up in a time when it was an offence to engage in sexual contact with another man. Gay men went to prison. Lots of people lived a lie because of it. I hid my sexuality and pretended it didn't exist. One good thing that came out of that was I married your mother, and you were born. And I'm glad of that."

I sensed Daniel wanted to protest, but then he backed down.

"We were so happy when you were born, Daniel," said Alex earnestly. "I did love your mother. Christopher told me that I owe you an explanation about why I left, and yes, I agree. I did something stupid that hurt your mother. I went behind her back with a guy at work. It was only once, but after that happened, I knew I couldn't stay at home with you or Joanna. So, I took the job in the States."

Daniel's face remained neutral after he had heard this revelation. I guessed nothing surprised him anymore. "Did Mum know about this man?" he asked.

"I told her after I was in the States. I was a total coward," Alex admitted. "I think that's probably why she withheld my contact details from you, Daniel. I swear I didn't know she was doing that. I would've tried to make contact with you another way, had I known. I just thought you didn't want anything to do with me."

"Well, I guess that's one part of the puzzle solved…" answered Daniel.

Alex leant forward and placed a hand on Daniel's knee. "Look. I'm not proud of myself for what happened, but it opened my eyes to who I really was, and part of me imagines how much worse it could have been carrying on living a lie, for all of us. I would have resented myself and Joanna. It would have been horrible for you to grow up in that environment."

Daniel shook his head dismissively. "Well, as it turned out, my life also had some pretty shit moments, too, moments when I could have done with a dad. I didn't have a great first experience, not like you sneaking off with some bloke from the office."

It was clear that Daniel was not going to forgive his father that easily. Alex sighed and removed his hand from Daniel's knee. He glanced up at me as I got up and walked away, leaving them alone. Part of me was still annoyed with Daniel. How dare he seek refuge with Jonas? Anything could have happened. Jonas was the type to prey on the vulnerable. It was not the time to bring that up, though. I suspected Alex would be devastated, too, hearing about what had happened to Daniel.

Hearing Alex talk about his divorce reminded me of a fantasy that I had occasionally played around with, imagining what it would have been like to have had a different father. I didn't know why I did this. I suppose, before my parents died, the main event in my life had been coming out as gay. I doubted either of my parents had ever thought about the importance of how I perceived their reaction. I had always reckoned that my father was disappointed, or that I had let him down in some other way. I knew my mother had reconciled herself to the fact she would never become a grandmother. The realisation I was gay had been eating away at me for a number of years, and telling my parents was in some way validating for me. I was not ashamed and never had been, but part of me wished my father had ranted and railed against me. That just wasn't in his nature. He was meek, something that infuriated my mother.

Once, when I was at junior school, my mother had actually left my father for a couple of months. It was never official. She just went to stay with her sister for a while. I didn't know what had happened, if there had been an infidelity. I had clear memories of my father picking me up from school during that period and preparing basic meals for the two of us in the evenings—meals my mother would have been horrified to serve to anybody. Happily, she eventually returned, and life carried on as if nothing had ever happened. I was too young to know, but whatever secrets were there had now been buried with them both.

Chapter Twenty

Now that everything was out in the open, father and son were getting on better. Daniel was back to his smiling self. It was still early days, but things looked promising. Alex even announced he was taking two days off work so that we could all go to Palm Springs. Daniel was pleased that Alex wanted to spend time with us rather than hide away in his office, but it still struck me that Alex might have an agenda. We left for Palm Springs the following morning.

"I booked us into a cool motel. You'll love it. I love this city. It has everything," assured Alex.

As we drove through Palm Springs, everything seemed immaculate on the surface. Manicured lush green parks and golf courses were peppered with small rainbows as the sun shone through the water sprinklers. It looked like a kind of paradise.

We arrived at the motel, which was an exact replica of one from the sixties. We parked by a huge red neon sign that spelled out the name of the inn. Our room was kitted out with everything we might need. I was particularly glad of the air-con, as the day was unbearably hot and stifling.

As we ate dinner that evening, the conversation steered towards Alex's experiences growing up. He said he had come from a humble background, but he'd glossed over the details. I suspected it had plenty to do with his drive and ambition in later life.

"How old were you when you first realised you were gay?" Daniel asked.

Alex looked around, perhaps in case anybody had overheard. "I was twelve," he said. "I obviously hadn't had any experience, but somehow I just knew. Was it similar for you, Christopher?"

I nodded. "Yes, maybe eleven or twelve, and like you said, I knew there was something different about me."

"I was thirteen," said Daniel. "It was the year before you moved out. I felt confused by it all, though."

"How come you never told your mother?"

"I kidded myself it was just a phase. That's why I didn't say anything. It was only at university that I knew for sure. I came out while I was there. I'd heard horror stories in the past of people coming out to their parents and then being shunned. I was always unsure what her response would have been."

"Joanna would never have done that," said Alex.

"Well, I'm glad I didn't tell her. I'm sure having her husband and only son both come out as gay would provoke some sort of reaction."

"When you were a baby, part of me hoped you weren't going to turn out gay."

"Why?"

"Because I had been unhappy for most of my life, and I didn't want that for you."

Seeing them grow closer reminded me of how the bond between my own father and me had lessened as we had grown older. Gone were the stories in the park. Instead, Dad busied himself in the garden or down the allotment. Gardening was as much a solitary pursuit as reading. It suited Dad. Our garden at home was always ablaze with colour, and looking back now, I wish I had taken more of an interest. It could have been something we had done together, as father and son.

Alex and Daniel could rebuild what they had missed and make up for lost time. The recent revelations might even bring them closer. For me, though, seeing them together reinforced the stark reality that my parents were never coming back. I needed so badly to blame someone for the fact Mum and Dad were dead, someone to shout at and rail against the injustice of it all. It seemed ironic that the one person who I now cared about the most could easily be taken away from me by his own parent.

* * * *

Even though we'd had plenty of days by the pool since we arrived in LA, the itinerary of the trip, not to mention the drama, was starting to exhaust me. Driving everywhere was also taking its toll. I was used to walking around to get to places in Bath. I fell asleep in the car as we drove back to Calabasas after Palm Springs. The heat and the drone of the tyres on the freeway had lulled me to sleep. When we arrived back at Alex's, I groggily dragged myself out of the car.

"Don't forget we've got the opening of Jonas' exhibition downtown later," Alex reminded us.

I groaned inwardly.

"I'm looking forward to seeing Jonas' show. Luis keeps telling me how impressed he is with his creations." I tried not to catch Daniel's eye as Alex continued to rave. I hoped the work on display would be pretentious and crude and that the exhibition would be a complete failure.

We were soon back in the car, driving to the exhibition. Alex promised we would grab something to eat afterwards, as there wasn't time before, which irritated me further. The gallery was illuminated on the outside with roaming spotlights, a flashy display which made it seem more like a movie premiere than an art exhibition. There was a long line of people waiting to go in. Alex spoke to the security guard at the door, who unclipped the velvet rope and let us through.

An impressive circular bar sat in the middle of the vast gallery space. All the walls were adorned with paintings, and the floorspace held plinths with sculptures. People clustered around the pedestals, sipping wine, studying the pieces intensely from all angles. Even from the first glimpse, I could see why the exhibition was attracting the queues.

A waiter appeared with a tray of champagne. I passed a flute each to Daniel and Alex and plucked two for myself, figuring I might as well have a few drinks if I was going to pretend to enjoy myself. I downed the first one and placed the glass back down on the tray, much to the surprise of the waiter. I thought I might have breached gallery etiquette. At the bookshop's events, I was always amused at how many glasses the guests would drink. Free booze was free booze. The mentality of it had caught up with me, after all. Maybe it was an English thing, or maybe I just didn't care how I behaved anymore.

Alex wandered off to study some pieces on a nearby wall, and Daniel guided me by my elbow, saying, "Let's have a look around."

We slowly circuited the gallery. I judged the shallowness and the vanity in the room, and it pained me. As we moved from piece to piece, I could admit to myself that Jonas was very talented, something Daniel confirmed. "He's good, isn't he?" He pointed at one painting. "I could see this piece on your lounge wall back in the flat."

Over my dead body.

"Oh look, there's Jonas. I'm going to say hi. Are you coming?" Daniel asked.

"In a second." I pretended to look more closely at the painting in front of me, but really, I was watching as Daniel moved towards Jonas, who was in his element, surrounded by a crowd of admirers.

"You look like you're at the dentist waiting to have a tooth pulled out." I jumped a little as Luis appeared at my side.

"Sorry," I replied. "Am I that transparent? I'm not good at these highbrow art things. I prefer book readings."

"It's the people who turn these art events into pretentious performances," he said. "Jonas needs them if he's going to get his name out there, even though the art speaks for itself."

"It really does." I couldn't lie.

Luis accepted two glasses of champagne from a waiter and passed one to me. We clinked the flutes together.

"To be honest, I'd also rather be at a book reading right now." He planted a dry peck on my cheek and wandered off. I wasn't sure if he had said that for my benefit. Either way, it made me relax a little. He was swallowed up by a group of people who greeted him with hugs and air kisses. I downed the rest of the champagne and spent the next half hour walking around the room again and again, people-watching and growing more pissed off. I refused to look at the art anymore. It wasn't as elegant as Luis' work, and the colours weren't as engaging. Who was I kidding? I was just trying to find flaws.

I didn't belong here. I was a charlatan out of his depth. I thought of Owen from the pub back home. He would be in his element. I could picture him proclaiming which pieces he hated while helping himself to champagne and shamelessly flirting with all the men. He would inevitably cause a scene, but it would have been worth it just to see him put Jonas in his place. I smiled for the first time that evening, picturing the havoc.

I swiped and downed another glass. It felt good, and I went to seek out even more. With a full glass in my hand, it was time to find Daniel. Alex and Luis were at the bar with a group of others. I avoided them and rushed to the back of the room, bumping into an older woman and spilling champagne down the back of her dress. I mumbled a quick apology and carried on before she had a chance to protest. I could feel her glare from behind me, and I giggled to myself. Up ahead I saw the back of Jonas' head. He was talking animatedly to a group of admirers. Daniel, next to him, was enraptured.

As I walked closer, Jonas was saying, "So, yes, a lot of my previous work was inspired by American art, but for this exhibition, I allowed European art to influence me, to guide me, if you like. I didn't really have a choice." He let out a self-conscious laugh, and everyone else laughed too. Jonas then placed an arm around Daniel's shoulder. "Speaking of Europeans, I'd like you to meet Daniel. He's my blond English prince."

There was a loud smash. Everyone turned to look in my direction, their faces turning to horror. I turned to see glass on the floor. I could make out a limb, maybe two, glistening, the splinters and shards glittering all around. It was the figurine of a pirouetting dancer I had admired earlier. Was it me who had knocked it clean off its plinth? There was no one else near it. Jonas' face filled with fury and Daniel looked mortified. He rushed over to me.

"What have you done?"

We both looked down at the shattered figurine.

"Actually, I think it looks better now than it did before." I giggled.

A hand gripped my arm.

"I think I'm going to be sick," I mumbled.

My stomach started to revolt as I was dragged away. Then I was in a cubicle just as my stomach contracted, bringing up all the champagne I had consumed. When I was finished, I stayed still for a moment, out of breath, hating the taste of bile at the back of my throat. I turned around to find Luis standing behind me.

"I told you I couldn't stomach art exhibitions," I told him.

"You broke one of his pieces."

"I know. I'm sorry. I'll pay for it." My stomach lurched, and the acidic taste of watery vomit filled my mouth. I spat into the bowl of the toilet.

"I doubt you could afford it."

He leaned over and helped me up, flushing the toilet. We then walked over to the sink, so I could splash my face. I caught sight of myself in the mirror. I looked appalling.

"Was it an accident, Christopher?"

I met his gaze in the mirror. I couldn't quite bring myself to look at him directly. "I'm not that cruel or vindictive."

He took a long pause then exhaled. "I know," he said with confidence.

* * * *

I awoke on Saturday, surprisingly okay physically, although my pride was damaged. I was embarrassed and mortified as I replayed what I remembered of the previous evening's events. After being sick in the restrooms, the last thing I recalled was Daniel helping me get undressed and pushing me into bed.

I got dressed and went over to the main house to begin my apologies. Alex was very forgiving and blamed it on the fact we hadn't eaten before we had gone to the exhibition. Daniel, however, was clearly annoyed. I had embarrassed him in front of all those people. Later that afternoon, Luis arrived in a huge old two-door sedan convertible with the top down. I was mortified to see he had brought Jonas with him.

I felt conflicted. While I wanted to apologise, I also wanted to confront him in private about the night he had let Daniel stay over. Daniel rushed to greet them both, but I hung back, pretending to inspect the pale blue 1950s Buick, which looked better suited to the streets of Havana.

I ran my hand over the curves of the metal, which was hot to the touch. Jonas swung out of the Buick theatrically. He was wearing loose cotton trousers. It was clear he wasn't wearing any underwear and didn't care who knew it. I strode over to him and held out my right hand.

"I owe you an apology. I'm so sorry about last night…"

He looked at my hand and, for an instant, I thought he was going to refuse it, but his stern face broke into a toothy grin. He shook my hand firmly. He was stronger than I had thought.

"To be honest, Chris, I never really liked that piece anyway. Thanks for becoming my new art critic. I'm going to use the pieces for a new sculpture, a deconstruction of dance."

I couldn't have hated him more. Why did he have to be so damn reasonable? I was sure this was all part of his act. Still, this small gesture relaxed the atmosphere, and Daniel smiled at me and squeezed my waist. I was overcome with pride at his display of affection in front of Jonas. It felt as if I had won.

Alex had gone to work, so the rest of us went out in the Buick. Luis took us to the Huntington Library, a sprawling estate spread out over two hundred acres. It housed several million items that went back to the eleventh century. As a history graduate, Daniel was eager to explore the corridors and drifted off with Jonas. I stayed with Luis, content to get an unofficial guided tour. He pointed out first editions and manuscripts by Chaucer, Twain and Blake. We went to the European art gallery, a sea of drawings, sculpture and paintings laid out before us. Luis was particularly drawn to Gainsborough and Turner, admitting his love of European art far eclipsed that of American. It made me realise half the things I'd heard Jonas say about art were just him stealing opinions from Luis.

Daniel and Jonas caught up with us after an hour. I wondered what they had been up to. They were laughing and acting like a pair of mischievous schoolboys. After lunch, we headed west to the Santa Monica pier and walked along the thick sun-bleached planks, letting the noise and smells wash over us. People hawked their wares from concession stands and children shrieked from the amusement park. A Ferris wheel dominated the view towards the end of the pier. The seats, painted red and yellow, looked like small rowing boats. Luis insisted we take a ride, and moments later, we were all giggling like kids, high on being young again. Jonas used my camera to take pictures of Luis, Daniel and me. Back on the ground, Daniel bought candyfloss, the sickly-sweet taste reminding me of my boyhood.

Chapter Twenty-One

Alex wanted to give us a tour of his offices and research labs, but I could think of nothing worse. Daniel, on the other hand, seemed enthralled by the idea, even though the whole thing was clearly Alex feeling guilty for being at work for most of the week.

"It would be good to see what you actually do," Daniel said.

I managed to talk my way out of the trip, insisting that they use the time for some father-and-son bonding, but the truth was I needed to be by myself. They had not long been gone, and I had settled by the pool, when Luis appeared. He insisted on taking me out to look at bookshops. I felt mildly irritated that Alex had filled my time for me, even though I hadn't asked him to.

We walked into the grand foyer of Barnes & Noble. The original gilded-glass ticket-booth of the former cinema theatre was still looking new. On the walls, in the spaces where movie posters would have been, were now adverts for paperbacks. Ornate designs still graced the ceiling, while the original screen and projectionist booth also still remained.

"Isn't it amazing?" said Luis. "Those are the original Art Deco lights on the walls. The theatre's been here since the late thirties. It only closed a few years ago. I love that they kept the original features. At night it's all lit up outside."

I surreptitiously took pictures, keeping my camera low. I had to show this place to Art. Wandering around, I took in any idea I could for the bookshop back home. As we left the old movie theatre, I took one last picture from outside. Luis listened as I told him about the bookshop back in Bath, which seemed a world away to me at that moment. Our next stop was a specialist store that dealt in art books. We left fifteen minutes later after Luis had bought a couple of bags' worth.

"Don't tell Alex," he said. "He'll kill me if he finds out how much I just spent."

"It's your money, though?"

"True, but he thinks some of the books I like are overpriced."

I thought of the expensive and less useful objects in Alex's own home.

Next, as we drove to West Hollywood, I found myself imagining this lifestyle. If, and when, we grew old together, would Daniel also berate me for buying indulgently expensive books?

We parked on Santa Monica Boulevard and walked towards a small building on the right.

Inside, gay fiction and poetry packed the floor-to-ceiling shelves. Academic volumes on queer theory and women's studies also filled sections, while biographies and publications on travel, transgender couples and erotica nestled in between. I ended up buying eight novels, hoping Daniel had room in his luggage to accommodate them.

We strolled the Boulevard, stopping at a café, where I told Luis about the books I loved. I felt proud when he told me he had read some of them, too.

"So did Alex and Daniel talk about what happened in Laguna?" he asked.

"It was slightly more than a chat," I replied. "It was a showdown. Daniel stormed out again."

"He seems to do that a lot, I've noticed." Luis raised an eyebrow at me. "So where did he go? It's not like he knows anyone around here."

I picked at the bread the waiter had left for us on the table and focused on tearing it into small chunks. "Well, as it turns out, he stayed with Jonas."

"I see…"

"He really upset me by walking out, let alone going to Jonas. I don't understand why he would turn his back on me, when all I've ever done is be there for him."

"To be honest, Christopher, I doubt he was thinking clearly. It sounds like he was reacting to Alex and not you."

I felt like he was slamming me down. "Yes, but why go to Jonas?"

"Because he could, nothing more complicated than that. What are you worried about? Don't you trust him?"

"I do. But I don't trust Jonas, especially knowing how vulnerable Daniel can get. Daniel said nothing happened and that he slept on a sofa."

"So trust him then. Look, Christopher, what's this really about?"

I decided I had nothing to lose, but I was somewhat superstitious about saying these words out loud, just in case I somehow manifested something. I had always stored my emotions in a box and hidden them away.

"I tend to push people away if they get too close," I began. "I've been hurt a couple of times since my parents died a few years back, but now I think I've finally met someone who I want to share the future with. It's a scary thought, but I'm willing to make that leap with Daniel. But since arriving in LA, it looks like that could all be taken away from me."

"Why's that?" Luis asked, watching me with curiosity as I decimated the bread into crumbs.

"Daniel would easily embrace the lifestyle here. Alex is successful and has an amazing house. Who wouldn't love the beaches and living in paradise?"

"Well, there's more to life than that, no? But you're worried he's going to leave you for a new life?"

"There's a possibility he's thinking about it..."

"Alex is a permanent resident, so Daniel could apply for a green card, I guess."

It was as if he were preparing me. Had Alex already discussed this with Luis? I felt a panic rising, and Luis reached out across the table to grip my hand.

"Listen," he said. "In the short time I've known you, all I've heard from Daniel is how great you are. Do you really think he would throw that away for a bit of Californian sun? If he did, he'd be a bloody fool."

"I don't know..." I knew he was trying to reassure me, but I was also aware that he was powerless to help.

"You can't walk his path for him, but you can walk alongside him. In fact, from what I've seen, you've already started."

"I love him," I said. "He's all I want in my life right now."

"You need to remember this isn't about you. It's about what's best for Daniel. Maybe he needs his father in his life right now."

I knew I was being selfish. It just seemed so unfair that I might lose him through no fault of my own. Luis dropped me off at Alex's, and I entered the house feeling like an intruder. It didn't feel right for me to be here alone. After a while, Daniel returned to the guest cottage.

"Good day at the office, dear?" I asked.

He smiled. "It was pretty damn impressive, yes. I thought Dad just had an office somewhere, but his company is much larger. He has different offices in three different buildings. Then there's this research lab a few blocks away. It's got restricted areas that I wasn't allowed to see. There's a factory, too. I still couldn't tell you what he actually does, though."

He was like a kid, all wide-eyed and animated. I thought back to my conversation with Luis and imagined myself walking parallel with Daniel, but then saw him confidently striding a clear path, only to leave me behind and boxed in.

"Sounds impressive."

I waited for him to ask me about my day, but it never came. Instead, he said something else. "There's something I need to discuss with you, and don't take it the wrong way."

"Okay…"

"My dad has meetings in Phoenix on the day we're flying back."

I hesitated as he looked away from me, then continued, "He's asked if I want to go as well."

"You mean you go to Phoenix, and I fly home alone?"

"It would only be for four days. It means I get to spend more time with him. He said he could change my ticket for me. I just need to ask the restaurant for more time off."

"Four days?"

"I know it's boring travelling back by yourself, but I want to spend more time with him."

I sensed this was the start of something bigger, but the last thing I needed was an argument. I could tell there was more he wanted to say. Was there another reason Alex wanted to keep his son with him and away from me? I was powerless to prevent this from happening without it coming across as selfish.

"Okay."

"I'm sorry I won't be travelling back with you, but thanks for understanding. I would hate for our last few days together to be ruined."

He made it sound so final. I smiled, but inside I was feeling grim. This wasn't his fault, and all Alex wanted was to finally be a good father.

* * * *

The next morning, as Daniel called the restaurant, I hoped they would say no. I knew he would just quit if that were the case, but maybe having a job to go back to would be more of a lure back home. I mulled over the scenarios, stretching my arm towards the empty side of the bed, where the warmth of his body still clung to the sheets.

He came into the room, then stepped back into the doorway. "My boss said it was no problem, but I have to take it as unpaid leave."

I felt relieved. "So you just need to change your flight?"

"I phoned Dad, and he's going to do it." He pointed to my bag. "I was thinking, could I borrow your camera to take to Phoenix?"

"Sure." I felt happier knowing he had something of mine that was too precious not to return. He knew the camera had once belonged to my father.

We took a bus then the metro downtown to see what else we could discover in LA. I bought gifts for everybody at the bookshop, as well as a thank-you gift for Alex. Time was running out, and I needed to make the days count. Meanwhile, Alex also seemed determined, and suggested a trip to a winery in Santa Barbara. Of course, he knew the owner well. I tried to stay buoyant as we walked around the estate, but Daniel noticed my anxiety. On the way back, we stopped in Malibu so we could walk along the shoreline. The expensive houses sat impossibly close to the sea. The mismatched jumble of architecture, constructed from layers of glass, wood and steel, was ugly and jarring. No thought had been put into blending them with the landscape. Alex pointed out the properties to Daniel and showed him one he had considered buying. I looked to the ocean with its gentle undulating roll. It was unreal to be in LA, but the extravagance was now a façade that bored me. I missed home.

It was a relief when Alex left for work on Monday. This was mine and Daniel's last day here, and it was good just to be the two of us. We decided to stay in the garden, swimming and reading. I had already packed so that I could be with Daniel rather than fussing with chores. I was worried that my full suitcase made me look eager to leave, though. Later that afternoon, when Daniel was in the pool, I went back into the cottage to change my outfit. I wanted to look good for him. He had left nothing important back at my flat in Bath — there was no reason for him to go back there. Even though I considered it to be his home, he might have had different ideas. I needed to make a good final impression. I went back out to ask him to come to bed with me, but he was hanging off the edge of the pool, chatting with Luis and Jonas.

"What a surprise!" I said. "I didn't know you would be here today..." I tried to hide the disappointment in my voice.

"I thought I'd come up and spend the night. I'll be taking you to the airport tomorrow," Luis said. Jonas didn't acknowledge me.

"I thought Alex was taking me?"

"No, he phoned to say he needs to leave even earlier for Phoenix."

"I see... I just need to finish packing. I won't be long."

I rushed back in, and Daniel soon followed, dripping water onto the tiles. "I thought you had packed already?" he said.

"Nope," I lied.

I had tried to fit my new books into my suitcase, as I was reluctant to leave them with Daniel. I wondered about my dad's camera, too, having second thoughts about letting Daniel borrow it. Daniel had picked some shells for me on Laguna Beach, and I had left them on the bedside table.

"Do you need any help?"

"I'm just about done, thanks."

I chose two small matching fan-shaped shells and passed one to him, showing him its twin, before I slipped it into my trouser pocket.

"Bring yours back safely," I said.

There was no chance for him to reply, as Jonas had now wandered into the room. He took a good look around, his eyes lingering on the bed Daniel and I had shared.

"All packed then, Chris?" he said with a smirk.

I couldn't even be bothered to pretend, so I just ignored him. Daniel looked worried. I had reached my limit.

"We should let Christopher finish getting his stuff together," said Daniel hastily, shoving Jonas out of the room.

I sat on the edge of the bed and put my head in my hands. Everything was coming to a close too abruptly. Alex had dictated that we were all going out for dinner yet again tonight, to celebrate mine and Daniel's time here. I was the one who was leaving, though. I was even being escorted to the airport, to make sure I caught my plane on time. Jonas would then be free in his relentless pursuit of Daniel, while Alex could make sure he tightened his grip on his son. This trip had ended up being an exercise in duplicity. I wasn't even sure what Daniel wanted or where his loyalties lay anymore. There were just too many things that stood between us. I went outside to join the others to find Jonas had casually thrown an arm around my boyfriend's shoulders. Daniel jumped as he saw me approach, knocking over his beer on the table. He shrugged Jonas' arm off and set his bottle back upright. Jonas shot me a smirk and said, "Don't worry, Daniel. I'll clean up the mess. I'll go grab a cloth."

I followed Jonas inside the house, walking up the flight of stairs to the kitchen. "Jonas."

"Christopher."

He fixed his eyes on me with a suggestive look. I laughed.

"What's so funny?" he asked.

"You are. You're a fucking joke." I paused to let it sink in.

He grabbed a cloth and went to step past me, but I moved to block his path. "Listen, you little fuckwit. I want you to keep your predatory hands off my boyfriend." I knew I sounded just as possessive over Daniel as Oliver had back home.

"Oh wow. And how are you going to stop me? You know he wants me."

I could feel the pain in my palms as my nails dug into my flesh. "What the hell happened that night?"

"What?"

"That night he stormed out of here and went to your parents' house."

"Ah, well, you see, Chris. I never kiss and tell."

I moved towards him without thinking, seeing panic flash in his eyes. I had him pinned against the wall, my fingers precariously near his throat.

"Keep your fucking hands off my boyfriend." I squeezed harder with each word, then let him go. His skin was red from where my hands had been.

"Oh my God, you're fucking insane." He was out of breath, dramatically rubbing his neck. His entire demeanour had changed, and he now looked small and crumpled.

"Jonas…" I realised what I had done and stepped back. I was shocked at myself. "Oh my God, I'm sorry. Are you okay?"

"What do you think Daniel will say when I tell him about this?" he said hoarsely. Then, he started to smile. I realised he could use this to drive Daniel and me further apart.

"Shit, Jonas, I'm sorry,"

"You will be when I tell Daniel, especially considering everything he went through with his mother's asshole boyfriend."

It felt like even more of a violation that Daniel had shared such painful memories with him, when I thought he had only shared them with me. What else had Daniel told him about? I let Jonas pass as I stood trembling with rage, feeling appalled at what I had just done. I had never been violent to another person in my life, yet here I was. I did not recognise myself. I covered my mouth with my hand to suppress an involuntary sob. I willed for the day to be over.

Dinner was a bittersweet affair. Jonas didn't say anything about what had happened in the kitchen and, instead, used the knowledge to keep me in my place. This final night signified the closing of a chapter that was now peppered with uncertainty and conflicting emotions, although it was the beginning of a new chapter for Daniel and Alex. We reminisced about the trip and even found a little humour in all that we had been through. I wondered if we would ever meet up like this again in the future. I wasn't sure. Throughout the meal, Jonas chipped away at Daniel, wringing his life story out of him. I was uncomfortable watching Jonas take in every word. It was as if he couldn't get enough of Daniel. He knew I was observing and knew there wasn't a thing I could do about it. As a frequent reminder, he would rub his neck. I wasn't sure if that was for my benefit or if it was genuinely sore. He had wrapped a loose linen scarf around his collarbone, even though the evening was balmy. I was curious to know if he was bruised.

* * * *

After dinner, Luis drove Jonas back to his parents' house in Encino. I had graciously shaken Jonas' hand and offered him a platitude or two without looking him in the eye. I said goodnight and goodbye to Alex, inviting him to stay with us in England. He, in turn, said I would always be welcome to stay with him in LA. With our formal verbal dance over, we all went back to our respective bedrooms.

At half five the next morning, I dragged myself out of bed while Daniel took his morning shower. He had packed a holdall with enough clothes for his four-day trip. My dad's camera was also in there. I retrieved it and replaced the used roll of film with a new one, then placed it back in the bag, along with one of my recently purchased books. He might want something to read if the mood took him. The shower stopped running, and he came in towelling his hair dry. I slipped back under the covers without a word.

"So, you're not talking to me now?" he said.

"Of course I am."

"Are you angry at me for staying?"

"No..."

"You've been quiet all weekend."

"Have I?"

He buttoned up his shirt and tucked it into his trousers before bending down to put on his shoes. "You know you have."

"Well, you don't have the monopoly on moodiness, Daniel."

"Great. Thanks for that. Well played. We can't all be perfect, you know — even you. Don't think I didn't see you kissing that guy outside the restaurant a few weeks ago."

"What?" A vision of Henry flashed through my mind. I felt sick.

"Look. I'm going to be late. Have a safe flight. I've got to go," he said. He grabbed the holdall and left the room. The door slammed, and I was left with nothing but silence. I couldn't get my head around what had just unfolded. I was unable to move. I wasn't ready to lose another person I loved. I took one of his pillows and held it tight against my face, taking in his scent as I let out a bellow of rage, frustration and loss.

At nine o'clock, I was ready to leave. Daniel's case lay open on the bed. I ran my hands over the clothes that were folded inside. Their colours were muted without him wearing them. I patted my pockets to check I had my wallet and felt the twin shell. I placed it on top of the clothes in Daniel's suitcase and left the room, shutting the door behind me.

Luis was waiting for me in the kitchen. The journey to the airport was held in friendly silence, but all the time I was wrestling with my emotions. I didn't want to involve Luis. We arrived at the terminal and parked the Buick.

"I have something for you," he said, gesturing towards the glove box. I pulled out a slim package. "It's to remind you of your time here."

Inside was a framed picture of a pencil sketch. It was beautiful and simple, yet hidden within it were subtle intricacies. Luis had drawn Daniel and me sitting on a bench facing towards the sea—just the backs of our heads, unmistakably us. At our feet were the wooden slats of the curving boardwalk at Laguna Beach. It was better than any photo. The tilt of Daniel's head, which rested on my shoulder, made my heart ache. My eyes filled a little, and I hastily swiped them with the sleeve of my jacket.

"This is beautiful, Luis."

"I made the frame using a piece of driftwood I found on the beach."

I traced Daniel's outline.

"I'm guessing something happened?" Luis said.

"We had an argument this morning. He thinks I'm angry at him for staying, but I'm not. I'm just terrified I'll lose him. We didn't even say goodbye."

"So you had an argument, big deal. That's all part of being in a relationship. Having time apart is sometimes good. It makes you think more about what you really want."

Daniel was battling with twelve years apart from his father. He would only be four days apart from me. I didn't think I could compete.

Chapter Twenty-Two

At Bath Train Station, I was overwhelmed with relief. This was home, and it was familiar. Too exhausted to walk with my luggage, I took a taxi back to my flat. I needed my sanctuary. Ptolemy was curled up on the bed, and he let out a grumpy meow as I entered the room. I sat down and fussed over him for a while, pleased to hear his deep purr. I hoped he would soon forgive me for leaving him.

It felt good to take a shower in my own bathroom. In the mirror, a mournful man stared back at me with bloodshot eyes and a downturned mouth. The time was eleven thirty, but my body wasn't sure if it was morning or night. Still damp from the shower, I lay on the bed and drifted off to sleep. I awoke four hours later, feeling better. There was nothing to eat, so I got ready to walk into town, grabbing my reels of used camera film as I left. I could get the pictures developed within an hour.

With June drawing to a close, the sun and warm breeze in Bath echoed the Los Angeles air. It was tempting to visit the bookshop to see Art, but I didn't want to deal with any questions that I was not ready to answer. I stopped at a café and took a seat outside, before ordering a sandwich and a small bottle of beer. It had been a while since I had sat alone to eat, but I wanted Daniel here with me. I picked at the sandwich and drained the beer. When an hour had passed, I went to pick up my photos. The unopened packet of images weighed heavy in my jacket pocket as I made my way home. Just before Brock Street, I decided I needed to see a familiar face after all and turned around to walk the short distance back into town.

"Christopher! You're back!" Art moved out from behind the counter and came towards me. "You're so brown. How's Daniel?"

My forced smile failed miserably.

"Oh no, what's happened?" The concern in Art's voice was immediate.

"He's still in America."

Art flipped the sign on the door, then turned the key. "Whisky?"

"Yes, please, Art," I replied gratefully.

The musky odour of Art's office, though peculiar, made me feel grounded. He retrieved two glasses and a bottle from a cabinet and poured two generous helpings. I never normally drank the stuff, but this time I relished the burning sensation.

He listened to every detail of what had happened in LA, which culminated with my regret at not going after Daniel to say goodbye. I even told him what I had done to Jonas. It felt good to confess the incident with no judgement in return.

"So, when's Daniel due back?" Art said.

"Late Saturday, maybe early Sunday…if he comes back at all," I said morosely, cradling the glass in both hands.

"What are you going to do until then?"

"I don't know. I thought you would be expecting me back at work?" The thought of not having anything to occupy me during the long, drawn-out days that stood between now and the weekend was not appealing. I could already picture myself drifting from room to room in my flat, dressed only in a rumpled T-shirt and underwear. I would forget to eat, my belly full of self-pity and angst.

"I've got a better idea," he said. "Why don't you take a few extra days off and get your thoughts in order? You'd also be doing me a favour."

"Oh?" I said, setting the glass down on the edge of Art's desk.

"I need someone to go down to my holiday cottage in Ilfracombe. Check a couple of things before it gets rented out next week. Fancy it? You'll be saving me a trip," Art offered.

I wasn't sure if he was inventing an excuse for me to get away. "I'm not sure, Art…"

"Go for a few days, and let the sea air kick in. By the time the weekend comes round, you'll know what to do. Saves moping around back here." Art swirled the amber liquid in his glass, then knocked the contents back in one swallow. He grimaced.

I considered his suggestion. "Well, I guess if I left tomorrow, I could spend a couple of days there, then return to Bath Saturday evening to see if he comes back…"

"Sounds like a plan to me," said Art, smiling across his desk at me.

"I haven't been to North Devon since I was a kid," I murmured, as I tried to dredge up an old childhood memory.

"More reason to go then." He rummaged in a drawer. "Here you go. These are the keys, and I'll give you the address. Ring me when you get there."

I polished off the whisky as he wrote the details down.

"Go home, and get some sleep. I hope you hear some good news over the weekend." Art picked up his spectacles from the desk and put them on.

"Thanks, Art."

"Daniel has a good head on his shoulders. I hope he does the right thing." Art looked at me and nodded, before turning his attention to the papers on his desk.

I walked home, dejected and lonely. I even felt alienated in my own flat. It was my one true haven, yet I couldn't relax. I sat with a glass of wine staring at my father's pictures and a shelf that held some of his books, one of which was an atlas I used to read when I was a child. I used to be fascinated by the thought of faraway places, but then when my parents died, I couldn't bear to be away from home. I pulled two large books from the shelf and took them over to the coffee table. One was an atlas from the eighteenth century that my parents had given me for my eighteenth birthday, and the other was a book of maps of the United Kingdom. I opened the second one and flicked through its pages until I reached North Devon to see where I would be staying for the next few days.

* * * *

The next day I awoke, eager to start my journey down to Ilfracombe. As I left the flat, the phone rang, but I ignored it for fear of missing my train. I had been back in Bath for less than twenty-four hours, yet here I was leaving again. The first part of the journey was uneventful, and I read to pass the time, still aware of the unviewed photos in my jacket pocket. I changed trains at Exeter, then settled down for the next leg of my voyage. I set one packet of photos down on the table and opened it, careful not to stamp the surface of the images with my fingerprints. The first picture was of Daniel in Alex's pool. He was standing in the shallow end with his arms resting on the edge, beads of water trickling down his face as he smiled into the camera. This was one of the first shots I had taken. Daniel's skin was pale and had not yet darkened. Another picture was of him and his father at the Griffith Observatory.

I opened the second envelope, not ready to linger on any of the images or the memories they conjured up, but Luis' face beamed back at me, and I couldn't help but feel sad. I missed his presence and listening to him talk. Our parting at the airport had been tender. He had known I was hurting inside and had put an arm around me as he escorted me towards check-in. At the security gate, we had hugged. Would I ever see him again? I knew I had met someone who had made more of an impact on me than my own father had in the latter part of his life. It reinforced the guilt I felt for not engaging with Dad as I got older — another regret never to be rectified.

I paused at the next photo, taken by Jonas. Daniel, Luis and I held each other, laughing on the Ferris wheel. The sun illuminated Daniel's hair as it streamed out behind him. Jonas had captured a moment of pure unbridled joy. I put the photos away, all except for the Ferris wheel picture, which I kept separately in my book.

At Barnstaple, I took a bus to Ilfracombe. The bus wound through the town and dropped me off near the promenade. It actually felt good to see the ocean again, and I took in the salty air. The sun was glowing amid the cotton-wool clouds that drifted along. Across the nearby shingle beach, families picnicked and played Frisbee. I crossed the road towards Art's cottage, following the directions on a crude map he had drawn for me. There was a small harbour where some boats lay on the sand at angles after the low tide had drawn the sea farther out. They reminded me of discarded toys. It was a huge contrast to Marina del Rey.

Huge white cliffs soared in the distance, then vanished from view as I made my way farther inland. The map directed me onto a pretty street, where nestled in a corner was the cottage. I instantly knew I would feel at home in this beautiful little hideaway.

I spent a lazy afternoon familiarising myself with the cottage. As I explored the rooms, it occurred to me that although the rooms were tiny, this home had far more character and charm within its thick uneven whitewashed walls, when compared with Alex's minimalist antiseptic show house.

Early that evening, I walked towards the sea front. The scattered boats I had seen earlier were now bobbing contentedly on the water. I asked a couple of passersby to recommend somewhere for dinner, and they directed me to a cosy pub, where I was now listening to the locals banter. I was happy to be in the distant company of others and not engaged in conversation. The alcohol was helping ease my tension. A sense of calm descended upon me.

It was late when I drifted back along the empty streets, my head spinning from the local ale. I passed a red phone box and felt the desire to call someone, wanting some company. I pictured Henry's phone number pinned to the noticeboard in my kitchen. I struggled to recall the numbers. Did it start with an eight? Who was I kidding? It was late, and Henry was probably in bed, maybe with someone else. I remembered his muscular frame and felt a yearning to undress him again, admiring and caressing his naked body. There was no way he would travel down here at this time of night. Selfishly though, part of me was fed up with pining for Daniel. He might never come back, and why should I wait? As I weaved back towards the cottage, I thought of my lonely bed and wished I had someone with me, not just for sex, but for the comfort of their presence.

* * * *

I awoke late the next morning, momentarily forgetting where I was, but the cries of the gulls soon reminded me. Only Art knew I was here, and it was a glorious feeling. Downstairs in the hallway stood a grandfather clock. I retrieved the winding key, then, as per Art's instructions, opened up the round glass front to expose the clock face. The key fitted in the middle, and I slowly wound the mechanism clockwise, orienting the hands to the correct time. Ticks echoed from the wooden interior. The heart of the cottage was beating once more.

I walked into town, avoiding the souvenir shops and inflatable rings of the seafront, and followed a back lane instead. The number of shops increased as I strolled and looked in the windows, acutely aware that all I was doing was killing time until Daniel was due to return. I had not, and would not, consider what I would do if he didn't come back. Right now, I had no purpose and was suspended in limbo. I shook my head as if to clear it of thoughts. I didn't want to probe too deep in case I didn't like what was in there.

Back at the cottage, the afternoon passed as slowly as the morning had done, the shadows bending around the room as the sun moved across the sky. Eventually I put my book down and stood up and stretched. I wasn't sure what I wanted to do that evening, but I would need to eat at some point. I didn't want to cook at the cottage by myself, so I once more left the house. I had noticed a footpath with a sign marked "Hillborough" pointing towards the direction of the cliffs, so I jumped the stile and followed it. After a while, the coast path opened out, and I was standing at the bottom of the hill I had seen from the house. I started to make my way up steadily towards the grassy cliff top. The harbour and the town sprawled out below when I glanced behind myself. By the time I reached the top, I was breathing hard. The view was great. The sea sparkled gold all the way towards the horizon, while an occasional boat rocked its way across the waves as they travelled down the coast.

To my left was Ilfracombe, and farther out to sea in the distance was the island of Lundy. There were no other walkers coming up or going down, but this did not worry me. I carried on walking along the cliff top for about a mile in the end, mindful of the hunger that was swirling in my guts. As the growls grew, I pivoted on my heel and started to walk back the way I came. On my ascent, I had passed a weather-beaten bench that was set back a little from the edge, so I stopped here now to rest. The paint had peeled off years ago, and the faintest of flakes remained. One of the slats on the back was missing and another was fractured, bowing slightly. I sat down cautiously, but the bench seemed to be holding my weight. The wind tousled my hair, and I breathed in. It was good to be this high.

It wouldn't be long before other souls passed by, so I took in the moment while I could. At the base of the hill, a person was already approaching. For now, though, I had the clifftop and view to myself. I closed my eyes and raised my face to the sun that hung low in the sky, relishing the warmth. A middle-aged couple walking their dog appeared over a ridge farther along the cliff. They nodded courteously in my direction as they passed. I waited as they descended towards the town, passing the approaching figure halfway up the path. I turned back to face the sea, following the trail of a fishing trawler, the fishermen barely discernible dots.

A faint voice carried over the wind, just a whisper, then all was silent for a few moments, until I heard it again. I sat bolt upright. Somebody was calling my name. Why was Art here? The figure was now coming up the hill at a pace, but they were slimmer, more agile than Art. They were now closer and running towards me, still calling my name. The glare of the sun prevented me from seeing them clearly, so I lifted my hand to shield my eyes and moved towards the figure.

"Daniel?"

"Hi…" he said breathlessly as we collided.

I was fearful to let him go, so our words muffled as we embraced.

"You came back... How did you find me?"

"There was a note posted for me at the flat signed by Art. It had an address and the words 'Go and find Christopher' written on it." He grinned at me, his chest hitching up and down with the exertion of his climb.

I stepped back to check he was really there and that I wasn't going mad. A rush of warmth coursed through me, and my eyes started to fill a little. But Daniel was stronger.

"What happened with your dad on the trip to Phoenix?" I managed to say.

Daniel's face darkened. "I was just so pissed off and confused after leaving you behind. Dad didn't even notice how quiet I was being. Instead, he kept going on about his business and the plans he had for it. And don't even get me started on that tour of his offices and factory. How could I have been so blind?"

"What do you mean?" I asked, surprised by his sudden anger and the clench of his jaw.

"I thought he was just being a proud dad showing me all he had achieved. Then I realised he was trying to get me to join his company, keep the assets in the family, that kind of thing. Remember that dinner party? I think he was showing the investors that I was part of his plans."

"What? Even though he hadn't seen you for so long?"

"Yes, he had it all worked out," Daniel said bitterly. "He even had green-card application forms ready for me to fill out."

I raised my eyebrows, shocked at the breathtaking level of Alex's arrogance, although to be honest, none of this was a surprise to me. "I did get the feeling he was trying to keep you there…" I admitted.

"Yes. I know, and I'm sorry." Daniel reached for my hands and held them tightly. "It was clear there was stuff you wanted to say, and I should've listened. I told Dad I appreciated his intentions, but moving to the US and walking away from you was not something I wanted. He didn't react well, but all he said was he wanted me to stay."

"Did he say why?"

"Not really. Guilt, maybe. Or to make up for lost time. To get back at Mum? Because he thinks having a son makes him look good? Because he wants everyone to think he's straight?" Daniel shrugged. "I don't know, but he was really insistent."

"It would have been so easy for you to stay in LA," I said as the enormity of what Daniel was telling me started to sink in.

"Yes, he has the lifestyle, and yes, I'm pleased he has Luis in his life," Daniel continued, "but he genuinely believed I could walk away from you. I asked him if he would give up all that he had for Luis, and he wouldn't answer. I told him I wasn't going to make the same mistakes he made all those years ago."

"You said that?" I tried to picture Alex's reaction.

Daniel nodded. "Yes. He looked pretty wounded. Someone that successful isn't used to being turned down, I guess. Back at the hotel, he actually pleaded with me. When he realised I wasn't going to change my mind, he said he still loved me, and that was it. I took the train back to LA and swapped my flight yet again. When I arrived back at the flat and saw the note, I came straight down."

I smiled at the way Daniel made his trip back sound so effortless and easy. Impulsively, I hugged him again. As I looked over his shoulder down the hillside he'd just climbed, something occurred to me. "How did you know I would be up here, though?" I asked, leaning back to look at him.

"I tried the cottage first, but then I remembered that first time you pointed out your flat to me from the pavement. You said you like being up high, as it's a good place to think."

I was impressed by his good memory. "Yes, that's true..."

"And then, the first time I went inside, I remember seeing all the photographs on your wall. As I was walking up the hill just now, I couldn't stop thinking about them." Daniel stepped back and put his hands on my shoulders, gripping them firmly. His eyes searched my face. "I want a wall of pictures just like that, but filled with images of us."

We stared at each other for a moment, then his hands dropped away. I went back to the bench and removed my book from my rucksack.

"We can start with this one, if you like?" I handed him the image of us on the Ferris wheel.

We sat on the bench and looked at the ocean. The grass was faded at our feet from the countless others who had sat there before.

"I owe you an apology," he said. "I overreacted when I said I saw that guy give you a kiss."

"That was Henry," I explained. "We spent one drunken night together a while back. I just bumped into him by chance that night. I told him I was waiting for you, and he just kissed me goodbye, nothing more. I should have told you."

"It's okay. I saw what he did and that it had taken you by surprise. I just wanted an excuse to leave without it hurting so much, but it made it worse. There is something else I need to tell you though. It's about Jonas…"

"Don't…" I said. "It's fine." I knew if he confessed anything, then I would have to as well.

"Nothing happened," he said, looking hurt. "All I wanted was to sleep on the sofa. But he wanted to stay up and chat. I told him I was tired, and he left me alone, but in the morning he appeared in his underwear and tried to lie down with me. I just got up and left. He was fun to be around, but you never had anything to worry about, you know. It was always you."

Daniel's eyes looked earnestly into mine.

"I would never do anything to hurt you. You know that, right?" I asked.

He nodded, then placed something in my palm. A leather cord unravelled as I held it up. The shell I had left for him was now delicately hanging from it. He pulled aside the collar of his shirt to reveal its twin, suspended from a similar cord. He took the necklace from my palm and fastened it around my neck. The contact sent electricity through me as the sensation danced against my skin. Each touch felt like it was exactly meant to be. I kissed him hard, and we both knew that right here, right now was the only thing that mattered.

He broke away to let his head rest on my shoulder, and I put my arm around him. As the light of the day faded, the sun set fire to the sea.

Want to see more like this?
Here's a taster for you to enjoy!

Falling Hard: A Hard Sell
Jennifer Moffatt

Excerpt

Ding.

The elevator doors slid open and Luka Moreno bounced out, a ray of sunshine flooding the dim reception area. He paused when he caught a glimpse of himself in the mirrored 'Breakpoint Advertising' sign on the wall, straightening the collar of his checkered dress shirt. It peeked out from beneath his purple sweater and matched his navy trousers. His honey-toned skin was glowing. He grinned at his reflection. Sometimes, he just killed it.

A rhythm thrummed through his veins as he strutted down the hallway, drumming the beat on his thigh. His first stop was his best friend's office. He poked his head in. "Morning, gorgeous."

Tawney looked up from her desk where she was highlighting a report, markers in three different colors clutched in her hand. "Hey, cutie."

He blew her a kiss and continued down the hall, throwing a smile at the adorable rumpled sandy-haired hottie from IT. He didn't pause to say hi, though, because Luka was fairly certain that particular hottie was straight, and, even if he wasn't, Luka was not going to date anyone from work. Not again, anyway.

Luka waved at the colony of interns scurrying to and fro in the bullpen and exchanged pleasantries with the other designers as he passed their desks.

"Did you get my email, Luka? I'm dying to know what you think!"

"Moreno! I saw your new soft drink spot last night. You killed it!"

"Luka, I'm making an iced coffee run, you want?"

He grinned and winked and demurred his way through the pack until he reached his office and sank into his chair. The storyboards he was working on sat waiting for him in a neat pile. He'd have plenty of time to finish those up today, with hours to spare. Maybe he'd even get ahead on a few other projects, do some sketching or even inking if he was lucky. He could hardly believe he got paid to be creative all day, to turn his ideas into little packages of art for the world to see. It was a dream.

* * * *

Thud.

Luka looked over from his computer screen to the stack of files Tawney had just dumped on his desk.

"Sorry." She smiled apologetically. "For the new account."

Luka was unable to stifle a groan. "Ugh." He rubbed his eyes. "What time is it?"

"Almost eight. You should get out of here."

He pouted at her. "I'm not the only one still at work."

"I'm on my way. Wanna grab some food?"

The panels on his screen blurred as he blinked at them. His stomach was growling, but... "I said I'd have these storyboards finished today."

"You're still working on those? You were almost done this morning!"

"Well..." Luka gave Tawney a sheepish look.

"Oh, no. Don't tell me." Tawney folded her arms and glared at him.

Biting his lip, he nodded, unable to say the words.

"Luka! Why do you keep helping him?"

Luka moaned and flopped his head onto the desk. "Because I'm pathetic." His reply was muffled.

Tawney nodded in agreement, her tight brown curls bouncing emphatically. "Yes. Yes, you are. But so is Morgan. You need to stop."

"I know," Luka admitted. God, did he ever know.

"Because, once again, you spent the entire day doing his shit, and now —"

He interrupted her with a tortured moan. "It's okay, babe. I already hate myself." *Never* would he *ever again* date someone from work.

Tawney softened. "Okay, but don't stay too much longer. You need some rest. Tomorrow is a big day."

Luka looked at her, mind scrabbling for purchase. "Remind me..."

"You poor thing, it may be too late for you. The Big Bad Wolf, Luk! He's here tomorrow!"

Luka smacked his forehead. "I knew that. Shit, this week has been insane. I *should* get out of here." He would just come in a little earlier than normal to finish polishing the storyboards. Because it actually *was* a big day. Thomas Badgley, a.k.a. 'The Big Bad Wolf,' was a company legend. A VP known for swooping in and working his magic for the major clients. And their office had just landed the Sartini account. It was *major*.

"Yes, you should. I hear he's intense. You don't want to be half-asleep when you meet him."

"I guess you don't get a nickname like 'Big Bad Wolf' by being a giant ball of fluff."

"Guess not. See you tomorrow, Luk." Tawney gave him a wave and eased out through the door. The office was dark, the empty desks and chairs now just humped, silent shadows. Last one out, again. Then his stomach growled, more insistent this time, and he decided that the smushed granola bar at the bottom of his bag was not going to cut it. Time to go home.

He struggled to keep his eyes open on the train, then grabbed an order of red curry from the Thai place he hated, just because it was fast and on the way. Luka dropped his keys on the side table, dumped his laptop bag on the chair then went straight into the kitchen to find a fork. A minute later he was digging into his dinner in front of *Breaking Bad*. He let himself sink into the meth-dealing shenanigans, his exhaustion temporarily forgotten.

But by the time the episode was ending, Walt's current predicament seemingly beyond hope, Luka's eyelids were drooping. He turned the TV off as soon as the credits began to roll, before the next episode could suck him in. He meant to go to bed, but somehow he found himself picking up his guitar from its stand by the couch. He plucked a few notes, a melody that had been winding through his head all day, the metal of the strings cool under his thumb. He strummed again, closing his eyes, letting the vibrations wash over him.

His mom had started teaching him piano before he could even reach the pedals, and the violin and guitar had followed soon after. Music was woven into the fabric of his soul, but it was a part he didn't share with many people. Not since the *Say Hi* Horror, anyway.

Besides his family, the only people who knew about his musical talents were Tawney and Finn. Though now, against his better judgment, Morgan had been added to that group.

He put his guitar back on its stand and went to bed. It took him just a minute to fall fast asleep.

Unfortunately, Luka had the annoying habit of waking up well before his six a.m. alarm. There would be a moment, usually around five, sometimes even earlier, when he became aware that he was awake. A switch would flip, and his brain would begin whirring away. Mostly things to do at work — *Shit, I never got back to accounting about the hours for the Boyer file. Is the meeting with the casting director at nine or nine-thirty? I have to remember to check with Finn about the font for the catalogue...* But there were other random things, too. *Did I have five cups of coffee yesterday? Is that too many? Do I need to buy more coffee? Ooh, it's my sister's birthday next week. Should I get her a gift certificate for a massage? Wait, is that what I got her that last year?*

Sometimes, just for fun, his brain would start flipping through the stack of index cards that meticulously recorded all the embarrassing or stupid things he had done in his life. Secretly fucking Morgan for months was at the top of that stack right now, and the *Say Hi* Horror always made an appearance.

On rare occasions, when he was really worn out, he would manage to shut all that noise down and drift back to sleep. Of course, then he began his day being jarred awake by the alarm at six. He wasn't sure which was worse. This Friday morning, however, he must have been extra exhausted, because for the first time in years, he turned his alarm off and fell back asleep without even realizing it.

When he woke up a while later, feeling refreshed, he picked up his phone to look at the time, then threw himself out of bed with a shriek. "Fuck! Fuck fuck fuuuuuuuck, fucking fuck!" It was 8:07. He was supposed to be at his desk by eight-thirty. That was not happening. Of all the fucking days to be late for work for the first time.

He dashed into the shower to scrub clean, then yanked on the first clothes he got his hands on. A bagel thawed in the microwave while he brewed his coffee, since there was no functioning without it. Then he was out of the door, travel mug in hand, swearing again when the coffee sloshed onto his shirt.

Collapsing into a seat on the subway, he texted his boss.

Hi Ilona – I'm so sorry, it seems I slept through my alarm, I'll be a little late…

He held his breath after he had hit 'send' then sighed with relief when it went through. His boss was beautiful, polished and more than a little intimidating. Some days he still couldn't believe Ilona had hired him, a fresh face with not much more than a charming smile and a padded resume. And that was when he wasn't running late for the most important meeting of the year.

Then the lights flickered and the train began to slow down, before grinding to a halt in the dark tunnel. Luka joined the other passengers in groaning loudly. How could this be happening? The speaker crackled to life and a disinterested voice explained there was a technical problem causing a short delay and thanking them for their patience. Luka added another text for Ilona, leg jittering as he tapped on his phone.

And my train just stopped.

This one didn't go through. *Fuck. No signal.* He sighed and pressed his head to the cool glass, willing the metal tube back to life. *Oh, God.* He pictured everyone sitting around the conference table, staring at his empty seat, Morgan as smug as ever.

It was an excruciating fifteen minutes before they were moving again. Luka had been starting to wonder if he could pry open the doors and climb up to a manhole cover, but that was rendered unnecessary when they lurched back to life. As the beleaguered train was finally pulling into the station, two messages popped up. One was a reply from Ilona.

Come to the conference room when you arrive.

The other was from Tawney.

Where are you???

He dashed up the stairs and sprinted the three blocks to his office, dodging cars and what seemed like exceptionally slow-moving foot traffic. Eyeing a crowd waiting at the elevator, he bounded up four flights of stairs, his heartbeat echoing louder than his footsteps. White spots were floating in front of his eyes by the time he arrived in the foyer, sweaty and heaving like a racehorse. He dabbed a sleeve at his forehead and made his way down the hall, attempting to get his breathing under control lest someone call nine-one-one on account of his imminent heart attack.

Pausing outside the conference room, he caught a glimpse of the packed space, all eyes focused on a person at the front he couldn't see. *Fucking. Hell.* There was nothing to do but go in. He took another ragged breath, smoothed his jacket then pushed the door open, oh so quietly.

Every head in the room whipped over to stare at him. Luka froze, an awkward smile on his face, determined to avoid making eye contact with a single person. Another bead of sweat trickled down his forehead.

"So sorry," he stage-whispered, embarrassment flooding his face. The room was jammed with just about the entire office, extra chairs crammed in another ring around the table and wherever else they would fit. There was an open seat right next to Tawney. However, it was on the other side of the table, through the dense sea of people. "Excuse me," he whispered to the first person he had to squeeze past. And again, "Excuse me," to the next. Every pair of eyes watched him in silence. *Fucking kill me now,* he thought to himself, mouthing "Sorry," again.

Seventeen million years later, he fell into the chair. It screeched like a car wreck. He closed his eyes, not quite ready to risk a glance at the head of the table.

"Well, now that Luka is settled," Ilona said dryly, "please go ahead, Thomas."

Luka dared to raise his eyes. Then he saw Thomas Badgley for the first time. *Oh…my fucking God.* It was like in movies when the rest of the world faded away to an irrelevant gray blur, and all that was left was one perfect person bathed in heavenly light. Luka was sure he made an audible wheeze, the breath he had barely gained back gone again. Tawney shot him a concerned look, but he didn't care.

How *could* he? Because Thomas Badgley was the most insanely gorgeous man he had ever seen in his entire life. It was impossible to look away. And Thomas was staring back at Luka with a smooth face and phenomenal eyes, a warm, shining golden brown. But just for a split second, then Thomas' gaze returned to the rest of the room.

Luka continued to drink him in, his mouth gaping. Thomas had wavy hair, a rich chocolate-brown, long enough to be pulled back into a small bun. He was at least six-foot-two, with ivory skin, a strong, chiseled jaw, a heavy brow and a wide, muscular frame that tapered into a narrow waist. His thick shoulders and arms looked ready to burst through his expensive, charcoal-gray fitted suit jacket. *Big Bad Wolf, indeed.*

Thomas was speaking, although Luka had no idea what he was saying. He was lost in the way Thomas' lips formed around each sound he made, the flashes of a pink tongue and the deep baritone of his voice vibrating the hairs on Luka's skin.

Then he realized everyone was staring at him again, right as Tawney kicked him under the table.

"Sorry?" Luka choked out.

Ilona cleared her throat and arched her eyebrow. "I was just saying, Luka has finished up those storyboards, haven't you?"

Fuuuuck. "Yes. I mean, no. Almost. The subway…" His cheeks flared up again.

"Hmm," Thomas grunted. He didn't look impressed.

"Well," Ilona said, shooting him a disapproving frown, "the design team can meet again later today. But I think the rest of us are clear on next steps. Thanks, everyone."

This time he caught the sympathetic glance Tawney threw at him.

Fuck me.

About the Author

Tom Crampton lives in the Georgian city of Bath in England, with his husband Charlie, and over 60 assorted houseplants. He first started writing during the Covid pandemic. 'A Different Corner' is his first novel.

Tom loves to hear from readers. You can find his contact information, website details and author profile page at https://www.firstforromance.com/

PUBLISHING

Sign up for our newsletter and find out about all our romance book releases, eBook sales and promotions, sneak peeks and FREE romance books!